Library of
Davidson College

# Alexander Suslov
# LOOSESTRIFE CITY

### translated by David Lapeza

ARDIS ANN ARBOR

*Alexander Suslov*
*LOOSESTRIFE CITY*
*English translation of*
*PLAKUN-GOROD (first published in Russian by*
*"Grani")*


*Copyright © 1980 by Alexander Suslov*

*ISBN 0-88233-468-9 (cloth)*
*ISBN 0-88233-586-3 (paper)*

# LOOSESTRIFE CITY

## CHAPTER ONE

Three suns rose over the city that day, and three slate shadows milled around everyone like paupers after alms, begging, demanding their due. The cats were afraid of these shadows and scrambled up the trees in terror. They howled and tore their wide sides on the branches. It was a holiday.

The holiday looked fervidly through the three suns over the city and cast three black shadows. The holiday was in a playful mood and playfully, suddenly, it banged the three suns together, banged them loudly in the empty sky. Crows rose from the birches like burning brands.

The holiday laughed. It came bowling out of the three windows in the sky, whirling and flying down the streets. It was a holiday.

The policeman at the crossing whirled too, beating off the hungry cars that howled like the cats in the branches. Stamping his boots, he also cast three shadows, and they whirled madly on the asphalt, battling the cars.

From the window of an old building whose gray corner faced the crossing with its chimney and rusty antenna, Marusia watched the policeman. He didn't seem very festive to her.

It was sad in the dark room. Marusia watched the policeman beneath the suns, and it got even darker. The pendulum ticked in its dark case on the dark wall, and the air was black in the room. Still Marusia thought that the policeman would smile at her pale face in the dark window behind the double frames.

How could he help but smile when she was smiling?

Marusia laughed as she looked through the heavy double frames with black, city dust and a paper flower between them. They had taken her voice, but they could not hold back that smile.

The policeman smiled too, just smiled at something to himself; but once he saw Marusia, he grinned beneath his cap.

"Hello, beautiful!" he yelled.

Marusia could not hear through the frames. She put her ear to the glass, but the glass shook from the cars racing by. She couldn't understand a thing.

Marusia smiled and disappeared into the room, but the patrolman stayed and battled the cars for a long time.

"Why are you sitting home?" grumbled her mother. "Young, and she's a stay-at-home."

Setting down her patterns, cut from newspaper, with folded workers and creased portraits of government officials, she looked at her daughter.

Her father was lying there, on the old sofa with its torn upholstery, reading the paper. What could he see there in the dark? Yet he grumbled something too and turned over, twanging a spring. A hum ran through the sofa.

"Or help me over here," her mother said, thinking better of it, and peering at the dark mass of chintz.

"Help your mother," growled her father.

"Later, Mama." Marusia was already standing at the door. "I've got to stop by my girlfriends'—after all, it's a holiday."

Her mother sighed and didn't say anything. Her father said nothing, crumbling down the colums of newsprint until he had vanished from the sofa with the spring and the hum.

The door slammed behind Marusia. The bell clanged in its dark, steel cup, and the blow rolled down the steps of the entryway. A dark entryway, even darker than the room. Marusia ran down the steps and slammed the door again, and the new sound darted upward with a springy wail. How nice it was out on the streets!

It was nice at her girlfriends' too—fun. Their hot faces flashed by, and they moved even faster in the kitchen, cooking. But it was nice in their rooms—clean, all tidied up.

The table was set in the big room. The napkins were puffed in cones, and the hors d'oeuvres set out: thin-sliced ham pouring a pink light on lettuce leaves with drops of cold moisture, the heavy glass of pike-perch in aspic with the frozen flame of lemon in it, and even caviar standing in damp grains in the quivering light. True, not much caviar.

In the corner, another table, smaller. There was fruit on it: bunches of dull grapes, peaches with a delicate, girlish down, and yellowish-red apples stewing in their own fragrance.

Marusia feasted her eyes on it all, pressing her cool palms to her flushed cheeks. It'll be dazzling fun! She set to work.

\* \* \*

The girls got dressed only towards evening. Three suns no longer burned through the window, and the asphalt lay like cold ash. The cats calmed down and softly, stealthily scattered across the lawn. One moon shone like ice in the sky and lighted two little stars with a spark.

The bell clanged in the hall, and the fellows came

in—in ties, all dressed. Lots of fellows.

"Hey, girls!" yelled Borka. He winked at them dashingly and started to open a black briefcase.

"Cognac!" someone exclaimed.

"Right you are," Borka confirmed, setting five bottles on the table at once. Wine appeared too.

"Efim, let's have some music," ordered Borka, snapping his fingers.

The electronic eye flashed green, spread wide and the music rushed out, hurriedly filling the room. The fun wavered and pitched, spinning in a bold whirlwind around the room, ringing in the glasses, rolling across the boys' slightly embarrassed smiles. Drunken, joyous fun.

The window opened wide. The moon shied from the fire of the brimming panes, and the music flew out, nearly grazing it. It raced down the evening street, echoing in the entryways and arches, rolling down the rooves. It was the holiday rolling, whirling and flying down the streets!

The couples whirled too. They were happy, and happily they whirled, gamboling in the blaze like maidenhair.

Marusia danced well, Borka did too, but a stranger, a fellow in a scarlet shirt, danced best of all. He came late, when everyone was already at the table. He brought wine too. Though no one knew him, how could they help but let him in once he had come? He looked at Marusia and laughed. He said something to her, and laughed whitely beneath lips scarlet as reflections of the silk he wore. And Marusia laughed ringingly— a handsome guy, how could she help but laugh?

An imposing fellow, well built, taller than anyone. He laughs happily, but his eyes are dark. He keeps asking Marusia to dance, he looks only at Marusia. Her heart starts beating. The girls see that and whisper to one another, laugh. Only Borka isn't happy, smoking in a chair in the corner, a ribbon of black smoke unrolling above him. A thin ribbon, just hanging there. Borka is sad. "What does she see in him?" he thought drearily. "Well, he's a healthy bugger. Is that it? He ripped off a fancy shirt, but just ask him if he's got a suit, I'm sure he doesn't... But them maybe he does—the face of a speculator."

"Efim," he called quietly.

Efim was dancing with a skinny, fidgety girl and lisping something to her—God knows what. She'll look up at him suddenly and then drag him aside somewhere and scrunch up her shoulders as if someone were tickling her behind the ear. Efim was content. And though it was far away, he heard someone calling him, and came over.

In the corridor they were hugging and kissing already. They had even turned out the light. It's dark—you go in, and there's just rustling.

"Ladies' dance," announced Efim, stopping the music. He waited and turned it on again, but stubbornly examined the way the cassette turned and the tape advanced, whished, and rewound. He did not have time to watch it down to the last turn. That skinny girl of his came up and asked him to dance. And Efim was dancing again, lisping, telling her God knows what. And she would scrunch up her shoulders as if someone were tickling her behind the ear. Efim was content.

The others were dancing. Marusia asked that guy to dance herself. Borka sat there gloomily, and got thoroughly depressed, so depressed that he stopped smoking. He really wanted to get out of there. But suddenly Irina came up. She was sorry for Borka, so she asked him to dance. Borka smiled unhappily and got up to dance. He was even telling her something, embracing Irina.

The moon no longer sailed, it clambered through the sky, leaning on chimneys like a beggar on crutches, caught in the antennas. It seemed that in a second the moon would start clowning around, that it would sing something, dragging a wild song after it. And then it disappeared entirely, rolled off somewhere. Look for it. Where could it be?

It got dark in the city. The two little stars lit up completely, crackling so quietly, like cellophane. An occasional lamp nodded its stupid head. And shine—how could it help but shine? It was so dark in the city.

"I've got to go, Marusia," the fellow sighed.

"What for?"

"I have to work early. I work at the *Beryozka*,[1] so you understand, it's a responsible position."

They turned on the light in the corridor. It rumpled beneath the ceiling and mouldered on the fellow's shirt. He looked sadly at Marusia, clearly he didn't want to leave. She was sad too.

"Let's go, at least walk me home," Marusia asked.

They went out into the night air, and the wind rustled behind them. The windows were dark and quiet.

"Marusia, darling," said the guy, stopping suddenly and embracing the hot girl, "I love you, Marusia, marry me."

He bent down and wanted to kiss her. Marusia got scared.

"What are you talking about?" She tore herself away, feeling his hands slide over her shoulders and brush against her breasts. "What are you talking about? I don't even know you."

A dim light was reflected in one of his eyes. The other was dark and looked at Marusia.

"What's there to know?" he asked, offended. He stood silent, and the light fell on Marusia. "Well, let's meet tomorrow at least. Are you coming to the dance at the club?"

"Yes." she agreed and hurried home. Otherwise he would come up to kiss some more. She ran away and was very sorry she had later. She was afraid the fellow would be really offended and not come tomorrow. And oh, did she want that guy.

\* \* \*

Her father was already asleep, tossing about on the sofa where he had been reading the paper. But her mother was sitting near the lamp, shaded with a piece of paper, waiting for her daughter.

"Thank goodness," she sighed, "you've come at last."

Her old face, sharp with worry, warmed. Her wrinkles dissolved, coming together in a wedge above her nose. Only her eyes sparkled.

"Go to bed, daughter, it's late."

She just came up to her daughter and saw—Marusia was radiant, and her eyes were all aglow. She sat down on a chair by the door and didn't even glance at her mother. She looked somewhere through the wall, across the street, beyond the city, dreamed of something.

And she said, still not looking at her, "Mom, someone proposed to me."

"Who was it?" asked her mother, worried again.

"Some guy, he was at the Snegirevs' today. Says

he works in the *Beryozka*."

"He's probably lying." Her mother waved her hand, and the air shook the paper on the lamp. "Don't listen to such rot. Where does he live?"

"I don't know, Mom." Marusia looked at her mother.

"You've absolutely got to find out, dear, or we'll get linked up with some convict. Then you'll have your *Beryozka*."

"How can I find out?" Marusia went behind the partition, all pasted-over with photographs, and started to get undressed. The dress she'd taken off whished softly, and the buttons tapped quickly when she hung it on the chair.

"I'll give you some thread I've got..." The mother came over towards her daughter and saw her, exclaimed, "What a beauty you are!"

Marusia was ashamed. She quickly threw on her nightgown, tugged at the blanket and covered up.

"Fine thread, like a web—you won't catch it in a door—and strong—it won't break. When you say goodbye to him, throw it round a button, and the thread will lead you to his house. Then you can ask the neighbors what kind of person he is."

"If he doesn't go by bus," laughed Marusia and closed her eyes. "Okay, I'll try it."

\* \* \*

"Hello, Marusia," he said, and his shirt blazed. The fellow was standing there, and though there were lots of people—everyone came to the dance—she picked him out right away. How could she help but pick out such an Adonis?

"Hello," she blushed, "I thought you wouldn't come."

"Why not?"

The guy was sort of surprised, so she understood he wasn't offended.

"I thought you were joking."

"Joking... what kind of joke is that? —I didn't sleep all night, just pondered over you, Marusia."

This "pondered" surprised her, but she didn't say anything. He looked at her strangely. And like the other night, the light reflected off him—the lighted stage, where some fools were moving about in a winey flush, tired of life and everything drinkable in it, and someone with a bald spot just showing through his thin hair. All that was reflected in one of the fellow's eyes. And the other was black and looked at Marusia.

"He isn't one-eyed is he?" thought Marusia, frightened, then immediately decided, "No, he's not one-eyed. He sees with the other eye, it's clear he does. And he's not squinty-eyed either."

Just then the fools on the stage struck up something fast, and bouncy. Racing ahead of each other, they tore off in the brassy sound of their horns. The bass hurried woodenly after them, and the drum thundered through, flogging them all.

After an especially loud beat, when the curdled drumhead was ready to burst, a ringing silence suddenly descended like a second, imminent blow. A man standing on the side just as rapidly and recklessly cried out, "Good evening, Comrades! The Committee Worker's Club[2] doors are open wide to welcome all of you who'd like to relax and have some fun. To help you spend your leisure time in a cultivated manner, we've got the vocal-instrumental ensemble Motherland here for you. Let's welcome them, Comrades!" He swung his arm in a broad gesture towards the fools on stage and was the first to start clapping.

Thunderous applause broke from the strong, slightly reddish hands of young men in jackets, joining the coquettish clapping of pale little palms with bloody nails.

The fools on stage were noticeably shy. They bowed in various directions and threw themselves into a fast number as before.

The strapping young men had chosen their girls quickly and in good order, like rifles from a pyramid. They were already dancing. Marusia was dancing too—with him.

"Marusia." The fellow looked at her, and though it wasn't what he said—he was telling her something else—she saw that he was saying, "Darling, marry me."

Marusia laughed, but her eyes melted into a dark liquid and begged, "Wait a bit, let me get a hold of myself."

But she was terrified, and something fiery was burning her hands—that shirt. In the blue air of the hall, just barely lighted from the stage, it burned, smoldered, and sizzled with the heat among the dark figures.

"Marusia, marry me."

From behind the rigid blackish-green sidescene stepped a woman, still young. She spoke in a thick voice, and, just as thickly and hoarsely, sang something about cranes, the brevity of love, and the cold of parting. Her long dress crinkled about her feet, rustled like rain across the stage. Marusia became sad and remembered autumn, how she would sit at the window and look, look through the slanting streams at the corner, at the policeman in his slicker, until night fell.

The song ended. They turned up the lights, which exposed the singer's desperate décolletage, in which her breasts jounced and suffered. That décolletage lured the glances of the sports-jacketed young men. An aged Motherland looked at her with the same attention from behind.

The woman grinned and winked at the hall and went backstage, jouncing her breasts even more and swinging her hips.

"And now, comrades," cried the man, appearing again from somewhere, "the border troops' Red Flag Band!"

Someone backstage started a defening whistle, and with the merry tramp of their polished boots, the frontier guards leaped out on stage, each with some instrument instead of an automatic. They immediately fell in and struck up something happy, extremely spirited, with deafening cries of "Ekh!"

\* \* \*

They parted late. The frontier guards had already disappeared down the long street, stretched out like a snake through the city. They left behind the smell of their boots and the cry of a stifled, nighttime song along the road. The club windows didn't shine through the blinds, and no beam from the open door cut the boards of the porch. It was late and the door was locked.

The fellow embraced Marusia and wanted to kiss her, but she tore away again. Why she didn't know, for she'd kissed Borka before, and she'd kissed other guys. She remembered the thread only later, touched the guy on the shoulder and threw it round the button unseen.

"Don't take offense," she said. "Come to our place tomorrow, I'll be waiting, come over."

So they parted. The fellow turned and walked away into the darkness. The ball jerked, fluttering and beating like a nestling in Marusia's hand, fluttering as fast as if her love weren't walking—but running. Though the thread was long, the ball was soon unwound, dying quite small between her fingers. Marusia waited a bit longer and then followed the thread.

A dark house with a black roof among the stars moved toward her and stepped aside when she turned the corner. The wind blew right in her face, it wailed quietly in the empty lane. Single leaves on the tree would move, something would whisper, and there would be only the wind again. The houses were all black, black hills filled the sky. Not a light, not a sound. No shutter creaked, no dog howled, and the silver leaf of the poplar flashed no light.

The moon came out, light as a piece of old curtain, all translucent. The whole blackness of the sky was visible through it. It just barely lit its own way.

First the thread ran down the lane, then it swung into another, even darker, filled with the same quiet wailing of the wind. It caught on a thick wooden fence rising in the gloom. A blind fence—no gate, no gap.

Marusia stopped. She tried to stretch up to the top—she couldn't. Out of the corner of her eye she noticed the black shadow of a tree. The tree was close to the fence and a branch hung over it. Marusia grabbed ahold of the branch and climbed over. She landed in some garden. It was completely dark. She groped her way along the thread among the trees. She'd brush against a branch, and the branch would rustle and shake, and Marusia's heart would sink.

Another fence. This one lower. Again someone's garden. She walked around the garden for a long time, and finally managed to find a path. The wet grass gleamed faintly in the moonlight. Marusia walked, the little thread hurried on. To the left—a black ravine. From the path the earth fell down the steep slope into blackness. Beyond the ravine, far below, stooped roofs, gardens gleamed in the light of the moon. To the right—a meadow.

The path turned, the slope and the ravine moved off. The meadow disappeared behind bushes. A church appeared. White, it looked blue in the night. The facets of a gold cross glimmered dimly, and a cupola quietly swelled, arched in the radiance. A belltower with a black embrasure, where the sonorous body of the bell weighed, looming, and the small bells hung like fragments of the big one. All this was quiet now. Even the wind was silent—it was left behind, caught in the gardens somewhere.

She went up on the white porch of worn, pockmarked stone and touched the ring of the latch. The church was locked.

She stood there a moment, then quietly came down and rounded the white wall through the grass, especially dewy by the cold stone. High above, in the thick blue of the narrow panes, the moon was reflected. It glittered, then disappeared in the deep embrasure. The window was high—impossible to reach. She rushed to another window, on the other side. A dark wall. A dense shadow covered everything, just the window barely gleamed, illumined from within. In the dark she stumbled against something—a wooden ladder covered with white spots lay on the ground. She put it up to the window, looked in...

In the middle of the church her suitor was eating a corpse.

\* \* \*

With one hand he gripped the black coffin, while he gnawed through the corpse's forehead. There was no blood, only the yellow, dead skin was torn, and a moist bone, pale-blue, stuck out, dripping lymph. He bit through one eyelid—and the eye was gone, while the other was open wide and gazed wildly upward, where purple flames seethed in the black density of the vault. The clothes of the Evil One blazed with hellfire, and red moved on the damp varnish of the icons, leapt across the floor, striking and glinting off the gilded stands.

The Evil One tore the white fabric of the collar and bit into the throat of the eyeless corpse with his broad canines. The bones crunched loudly, and the head turned to bury its gnawed face in the white pillow which instantly darkened.

\* \* \*

Above Marusia the bell struck—black bronze—and the cupolas whirled into the sky, throwing her on the ground. She didn't hear how she screamed.

## CHAPTER TWO

Dmitry strode down the road. He did not seem to be tramping the ground, but raising dust with his boots for nothing. He did not get any smaller, though he was far away already—Dmitry was going away. Going off to war.

With his cap he sliced a cloud, lit up from below the earth by a fiery ray of sun. He moved the woods aside with his shoulder—they reeled bluely. Her Dmitry. He melted in her eyes, spread in tears across the forest, mixed in the rumble from the red cloud. How could this be? Dmitry was going away. Going off to war. And she stood there and couldn't cry out and couldn't do a thing. It was her Dmitry!

Everything was muddled, and her Dmitry disappeared. He was so big just a moment ago—his head hitting the sky—and now there's no one there... And never will be. The tears poured down, annointing forest and field.

Never will be... The thunder groaned in the distance. It broke where Dmitry had disappeared. And Dmitry wasn't there. *He was not there at all!*

\* \* \*

The lamp. And the table. And the crooked door. Work, like the creak of rheumatism. Work in the body. No getting away from it, and nothing to feed it. Hungry, she creaks and tears the hungry body. There are no tears anymore—everything is drunk up—yet something crackles, cracks in half. "Everything for the front, everything for victory!"

How much time had passed? Who knows.

\* \* \*

The lamp. And the table. The lamp isn't burning. It does not shine warmly in its kerosene light. The table is empty. And at night—rain. It drizzles in the blackness, speaks to her in her husband's voice and sows a river from single drops. The river grows murky. What is that rising there? Not woe?

"Woooe," drizzles the rain and speaks. It speaks much that was never said.

She went out to the river once at night. It wasn't raining any more, but there, beyond that accursed forest, it moved, raised dust on the night road, like her husband returning. The river lay quiet and black.

Everything was quiet, but her husband was returning. Husband? No—rain with her husband's voice, with a quiet voice, like an open grave. "Woooe," drizzles the rain and speaks. It speaks much that was never said.

She stood there a long time. Her tears were sown and floated in the river. What will grow from them? She cries and kisses her husband. And where is her husband?

... Dark. The river lay quiet and black.

\* \* \*

People avoid her. They are afraid of woe, though they live in woe. Someone laughs: she misses her husband! Someone looks sternly at her: is she trying to spread panic? "Everything for the front, everything for victory!" They will still sow. Savage people, they live in woe and in woe they multiply.

The work creaks ahead. How long it creaks! Day burst in her head, raising high a gray pole with a crack and the loudspeaker's black nest. That pole rushed along, and the earth was bent, the whole street set up like a wall. And on the wall wicked, broken people were cast.

Are they singing? Hardly! They're listening to the loudspeaker's black maw shriek. And they themselves bark, howl in savage voices. "Everything for the front, everything for victory!"

Who are they? Why all this? What for?

The large, shaggy muzhik Front stepped out from the damp earth—there, behind the houses, beyond the empty vegetable garden. With his red mug, he reels, and clutches a drunken broad. Drunk with blood. That isn't Dmitry, is it? The broad drags herself along, barely shuffles. She drags the muzhik down too. She crushes people, presses in deep, and the earth swells, bloats with graves.

... Slowly, how long they walk.

The muzhik couldn't stay on his feet. He fell suddenly, and it smoked, blackened around him. A piece of sky was torn out above him. It disappeared.

How the broad howls now, how she throws herself on the dead earth. And the people around, so small, begin spinning about. They bawl even louder. And though she crushes them and throws down their houses, they rejoice. "Victory! Victory!" And more graves grow, though Front is no more. Only Victory remains.

* * *

The lamp. And the table. The table is not empty,

weighed down in the middle by a sheet of white paper, not even very big. A heavy little sheet, heavy with woe. Woe froze in a groan in the house. You could not stand, could not move. There was no light and no air, only woe.

Woe was there. Can you grow used to woe? There had been something else once. Now this had come. Come and frozen. Dark.

"... died bravely... his country from the Fascist invaders..."

There were not even any tears. Everything was drunk up, eaten by the people, the ones rejoicing beyond the wall."Victory! Victory!" Dark.

And the house shook—Victory had come. The flat door creaked and swung open. Dmitry in place of the door—crucified, so flat. On one shoulder, a shoulder strap, sewn with three pieces of thread—he sewed it himself—and on his left boot, a reddish stain, a sole like stone. He was pressed against the wall, and will not ever be torn away. Dmitry creaked wrenching his boot, and let Victory in—just her red mug got through. She shoved her hand in and lightly snatched up the sheet of paper which no one could lift. She waves that sheet of paper, rejoices. The black maw gapes and bawls something. A bloody mist moves turbulent through the house. "So bravely!" it bawls, "braaavely! Rejoice, woman! Rejoice children! Rejoice, all! Her husband died braaavely! Bravely was he eaten, bravely was he stuck into the earth, bravely!"

What? Who's sobbing there? Who's sobbing when all around rejoice? Spreading panic? "Everything for the front, everything for victory!"

What front?—The Peace Front. What victory?—

The Victory of Peace. Well, so what if it reeks of blood too.

The huge, shaggy muzhik Peace Front stepped out from the damp earth—there, behind the houses, beyond the empty vegetable garden. With his mug pale as yellow bone, he reels and clutches a drunken broad. Drunk with sweat and tears. The broad drags herself along, barely shuffles, and drags the muzhik down too. She crushes people, presses in deep, and the earth swells, bloats with graves.

She screams into the sky, so high, scraped clean of woolen clouds. "How many, how many more will there be?"

"Many," rang back. "Many fronts and victories. While there are men—there will be fronts. While there are men—there will be victories!"

The distance was enveloped in flame, and in smoke, the sky above her. Shaggy heads rushed through the smoke, and in the flame, feet tramped thunder. The black earth jerked and swelled, and a corpse arose—the First Front. He froze the sky in black decay, cast a black shadow before him. And in that shadow the others stood—the Peace Front and Victory. They took up everything and there were no people left.

They entered her house—the roof collapsed. They struck—and it grew dark all around. And the house slid into the leaden blackness, casting a few pale sparks. It slid faster and faster, revolved, and everything collapsed... everything...

\* \* \*

Slowly her eyes cleared. A sort of gray mist stretched before her. People's faces rocked and swam away, went off awry. She swam too, quietly, head first. Some twigs jingled and parted in the mist. A pleasant smell slipped by, blended, clinked—it smelled of flowers.

She opened her eyes—a hospital, everything white all around, and she beneath a white sheet. An old woman huddled next to her, a grayish little thing, but with compassionate eyes. Any minute now tears will roll down her wrinkles.

"Who are you?" she asked.

The old woman smiled, so sadly, "Your woe."

"Woe?"

The old woman nodded and sighed, as if she were sorry herself that she'd come, but what can you do, how could she help but come?

"Can I come into you now?" asked the old woman. Someone might see."

"Come in."

The little woman got up—you could just see her gray kerchief behind the bed—she climbed onto the bed, crumpled the sheet, crushed the pillow and disappeared as soon as she touched her. It got so calm. It grayed over inside her.

And just as calmly she thought, "Why live if Dmitry's gone?"

Long she lay, listening to death. She fell asleep as unawares as if she'd stumbled into the old woman's grey kerchief. Dmitry came. It seemed that she was free from life. Her blood did not weigh upon her like mercury, and her heart did not weigh upon her, constricted in her breast, stuck through with needles. She cries and kisses her husband...

The sheet lay calm and white, as if she really were dead. Only the wind in the windows trembled, leapt into the room and touched the sheet. Heavy—it won't move, it lies like white marble, lies frozen into marble.

\* \* \*

But that was the last time she saw her husband. Dmitry disappeared. He stopped coming to her in dreams, no matter how she called to him. Even the dreams vanished. They would scud past in shreds in the night and hurtle away through the wall, blue in the moonlight.

She no longer thought of death. She saw the field where Dmitry died. Where is that field? Dmitry's there. She'll find her husband, find his grave. And of death she thought no longer. How could she die when Dmitry was gone?

She wrote a letter. The letter went off like a scream, flew off like a groan. But can you hear one groan among a million? They answered her, so sternly. "Everything for the front, everything for victory!" They would even arrest her. Savage people, they live in woe, and in woe they multiply.

She wrote again. Again she waited. They answered when she'd even stopped waiting. They disclosed the place where they had killed him, and promised to decorate him posthumously.

... And she rushed to her husband.

The brown field billowed damply, sighed like waves. And the sun, cowed and small, hid on the very rim, frozen in the fog, stuck to the damp earth. A bird rolled along like a ball of dry grass. It hit the earth, bobbed up and hit again until the wind threw it past the edge of the field, where its light, trembling chirp disappeared. With a roar, a tractor shoved into the earth and crawled forward. Far away, small too, the last little piece of green field turned black. Everything will be black.

And suddenly something trembled on that little piece of field, something quite tiny, red, that recoiled in her eyes. The sun? No. A star. A star on the grave. Dmiiitrry!

She ran across the field, and clouds bounded in the sky. Her face got so big it was reflected in the damp earth, it was scattered over the whole field. And on the very rim, somewhere on her cheek, the tractor crawled forward. In a second it will cut into her husband's grave, hanging there like a precious earring. It will rip off that earring, send it rolling...

The driver saw her—he jumped out of the cabin. Young. His jaw dropped so in surprise that his cap barely stayed on. It nearly plopped onto the tarnished caterpillar track with earth on the metal.

"Hey, lady, what's wrong with you?" he yelled.

She did not notice him. She saw only the plywood star. Not reading the letters which were half-obliterated by rain, she threw herself on the green mound with its short dusty grass, trembled, pressed against it. She whispered something into the earth. The words went off into the deep places between the roots of grass and came back muffled.

The driver watched, and he remembered when he visited his father's grave last summer. He went with his brother. They were both drunk and did not grieve much for the old man. Actually, they had come to have a few more. Their mother had given them some money for this worthwhile enterprise. They drank up everything and sat silent, as is the custom. Then his brother rolled their father a cigarette and lit it. The cigarette lay on the grave, smoking nicely. His brother was amused at something.

"You had a drink, now have a smoke, Dad!" he said, and stamped his boot. It rumbled back so through the earth, that they were both scared, unsettled.

He stamped once more, softer this time, and again the earth quaked heavily. There is dreadful earth in the cemetery, earth filled with dust. The brothers grew pale, they sobered up and left the cemetery.

The fellow watched her, and now he thought it must have been his father speaking. He stood there a bit longer. Then he moved off somewhere with his tractor, and only the dust rose.

She whispered something into the earth. The words went off into the deep places between the roots of grass and came back muffled.

\* \* \*

She didn't even die when she had found Dmitry. How could she die if the school there was named after him, if they were planning to put up a monument to him? It wasn't certain whether they'd put up the monument or not, but if she didn't write, didn't ask, it was certain they wouldn't. His name and exploits would be forgotten. Who would remember if she were gone?

But now—the grave is adorned with flowers, the Pioneers mount an honor guard every holiday, and especially on the Ninth of May.[1] Everyone knows her here. They remember how she spoke at the school, how she told of her husband's exploits, how they furtively wiped the tears from their own eyes.

She was nervous then, for she had to tell everything that was frozen inside her, everything she had told to no one, everything you usually keep in your heart. And who was there to tell? To whom could she confide her feelings? Certainly not to Dmitry himself, who came at night like rain.

Dmitry. Just the name said aloud gripped her throat, made her shake with sobs.

It was quiet in the hall. A chair would creak somewhere and freeze, frightened by the squeak. And it would be quiet again. Two baskets of flowers on the stage. One batch red, the other lilac. A red curtain hung on rings and froze, would not move. And she in front of the curtain.

"Children." She looked at the Pioneers, at their clean, slightly pale faces and forgot that she had never had children. Besides, it was not true that she had not. She had. For how many lives had she saved by her labor. "Children, never repeat what happened, what we lived through. When you grow up, don't allow war to come upon us. We don't need fronts, and we don't need victories—it is bad. It is bad when there is peace, but when there is war, it is even worse."

She stopped short, afraid the children would not understand her, the grown-ups not allow her to speak. What faces they had, sitting there.

But she remembered how she had spoken in government offices, at all sorts of committees where it was impossible to tell the truth. She had to speak, or else they would not put up the monument at all. His name and exploits would be forgotten. Who would remember if she did not speak?

She spoke of her husband, of how he grew up, of how he always respected his parents. She spoke all sorts of things she did not think. It happened, and it was true, but is was not the main thing—that was not the point.

She told how honest he was, and brave, and how honorably and bravely he died for his country.

She saw that the grown-ups had calmed down, but in her heart, what she said covered Dmitry with ash. However much her heart squirmed about, she could not touch the pain, but touched softly around it, covered it with ash. And lightly, she told of her husband's death, as if it were not Dmitry at all, but someone else.

She calmed down, and she forgot. And from that time on couldn't remember at all what Dmitry had died for. But later it was apparent to her that it was impossible for him not to die. He absolutely had to die so that the enemy would not pass, so that the children might grow up.

She looked at the children's tear-stained faces, and felt herself a mother twofold.

\* \* \*

They elected her to the parents' committee. She could no longer imagine her life without the school. She spoke, she told of her husband the hero, and it was pleasant to observe how respectfully the grown-ups looked at her, and the children, lovingly.

Only at night, when she was left alone, and the rain rolled through the forest, she would remember Dmitry, remembered her husband as he was. And she would dissolve in tears, shaken with sobs. Speaking— what is the sense? She only wept and cursed her life. And she stopped speaking with her husband in the rain. But then, it will soon be twenty years ago—all the words were said so long ago...

\* \* \*

Dmitry came towards evening. He knocked hurriedly at the door and, not waiting for an answer, strode into the room. So happy, young-looking. But his eyes were a bit anxious. He wore a gray jacket a shirt and tie, and he carried a briefcase, obviously heavy. He smiled, and in his anxiety that smile seemed sort of impertinent. He sensed that and stopped smiling.

"Hello, wife! Well, I'm back. Don't be afraid, not from the grave. I've come from Voronezh. Though I should warn you right away, it's not for good—I just dropped in on business."

He stopped, put the briefcase on a chair. He took out a clear, plastic comb, blew on the teeth and combed his hair, looking past his wife at the mirror on the wall.

"What I wanted was this: we should get a divorce, or else, you know... It's just not right. Look how many years we haven't lived together, and we're still registered—that is a violation. What will people think?"

He paced up and down the room, glanced at the shelf and saw the photograph of himself, where he was young, smiling.

"Oh, great, you've kept it. I'll take it, or it could be awkward, you know. I've got a family in Voronezh, grown children, and here's this photograph. Why are you so quiet?" he asked, as if he were surprised. He sat down at the table and looked straight at her.

And she stood there and couldn't cry out and couldn't do a thing. It was her Dmitry! How could this be? —Dmitry has come. Twenty years after the war.

"So now you just stand there, stiff as a poker." He frowned, struck a match and lit a cigarette. "I'm not going to take any of your living space[2] —you can have it. And I don't need any of my things, so you can stop worrying."

He blew out some smoke, grew pensive looking at her. "Mm-yeah, you've aged..." And suddenly he grinned roguishly, "Though the boys still come around, I bet?" He laughed.

He stood up and reached for the briefcase.

"No offense, I'm kidding. I wrote up a little application here, and it says: 'In view of my long-term separation from my husband, I have no objection to a divorce.' And so on. That suit you?"

He said that and stopped. Silence froze like a gravestone in the house. She could not grasp the wall, could not stagger to it. There was no light and no air.

"Why?" moved in the silence. And apparently it was not she who whispered it with deathly lips. The earth, the whole sepulchral earth, filled with ash, full of human bones, sighed heavily, as heavily as if all the dead spoke in one voice.

"What?" At first he did not understand. And when he understood he jumped up.

"Why?"

"To hell with you!" He grabbed his briefcase. "I knew I shouldn't have come. Why did I bother?" And he rushed out of the house.

\* \* \*

What have they done to her? To live in suffering and take comfort in suffering. They took away her right to suffer, took her whole life—torment and fi- elity—and threw it in her face. Only mockery was left. How everyone would mock her, how the children would laugh. Where is her woe when even woe is gone? Where is the misfortune that makes day like night, made her into a shrunken old woman? They took everything. Where is she? And why!

Black bronze spun and beat in her head. The house pitched. And once it pitched, it could not stop. Her head beat again. Something snapped inside. It beat and wailed—it grew dark all around. The house slid into the bronze blackness, casting a few pale children's faces. It slid faster and faster, revolved. And everything collapsed with a last brazen blow... Everything...

## CHAPTER THREE

Marusia is scared. It is dark. She waits for the Evil One to call—she invited him herself.

# CHAPTER FOUR

Day blazed. It flamed like a candle. Iron walls, rusty in the corners, with screws and clamps, shivered, rushed around the city. And she within those walls—already insane. Savage by the look of her, with her teeth that had fallen out all at once, and the ash of hair that spilled from her head. And why!

The walls flew, hurried, they rushed the madwoman to the madhouse. The orderlies hustled. It is hard on your reason to be around madness. How can you protect yourself? With walls and iron. Faster.

But why were they hurrying if it was the cemetery they needed? For she was dead, dead twenty years already. How could they help but see? But they'd never guess—a stupid crew. If she's still on her feet, she must be alive, they think. But even her heart was gone. That very night after Dmitry's arrival, they had gnawed it out. There could not have been much left of it—one swallow.

They drive. She looks out—there's the home, lit up in the narrow vent. It rushes off somewhere. Then huge, it swoops down on you.

"A-a-a... what's that?"

No, she does not need medicine. She needs a coffin. But just a coffin? How much other stuff do you have to buy? And you will not find it right away. You cannot buy it everywhere. How can she lie here?

"Why?" she screamed at the orderly through the grilled window. And when he winced, she burst out laughing to the hollows of her pitted gums.

She crashed onto the iron floor, quickly stretched out, and folded her hands on her breast, just below the holes they'd gnawed that night. Dead—see for yourselves.

The walls sped, rushed along...

\* \* \*

"Hey, lady, quit clowning." The orderly banged open the door and came in after her. "Get up."

She lay there. She did not hear.

"Get up!" He kicked her feebly with his foot. "Who do you think I'm talking to?"

He touched her with his hand and felt the cold, the fierce cold of a dead body. He winced squeamishly.

"Well, the old bitch really did kick off. Brother!" And he shook his head, puzzled.

"Hey, Fomka!" he yelled to the driver. Fomka was smoking in the cabin and did not want to get out, though they had arrived.

"Yeah?"

"Come take a look—the broad kicked off."

"So what?" Fomka remarked reasonably, not moving and rolling his grey *Belomorina* from one corner of his mouth to the other as measuredly as before. "Pull her out if she's kicked off. You don't think I'm going to, do you?"

"You fool," said the orderly angrily. "Tell him a patient's kicked off, and he argues about who's going to pull her out. Don't worry, I can manage without you.—Brooother," he drawled again. "I'm going to report to the guy on duty. And you, you clod, taxi over to the morgue. We'll pull her out in a minute."

"The ass, he's still swearing." The driver took

offense, and stepped on the gas so hard that the orderly's coat, which was not too clean anyway, was covered with exhaust fumes. He drove off down the narrow road between the hedges to the low, poorly white-washed morgue. "He's a clod himself."

It was quiet there. The hedges stood gloomy and dismal. The grass bristled, dry, sort of rusty. A dull sun daubed at the muddy walls of the morgue and was reflected only a bit brighter in the truck's windshield.

"Anyone there?" Fomka climbed out of the cabin, slammed the hollow, iron door with a bang. It was quiet, no one answered.

"What a joint," snorted Fomka. He spit out the butt, took out a new cigarette, flattened the cardboard mouthpiece and lit up.

The door to the morgue was wide open. The stench and the damp carried outside. Steps of worn cement, blue in the half-gloom of the entrance, disappeared down below, where it was completely dark.

Fomka did not go in. He stopped in the light and yelled, "Anyone there? Brought some reinforcements for you."

The sounds rumbled. They rushed down until they echoed somewhere very far away, divided up and died away.

"What a stink." Fomka held his nose and went back to the truck. But then he remembered that a dead old woman was lying there, on the cold, ribbed floor. He did not like that, it called up disturbing thoughts.

He was standing pensively by the back door of the van, which the orderly had only half-shut, when he heard something. There, in the van. Shuffling on the iron floor. At first he was a little frightened. He snatched the cigarette from his lips and opened his mouth, listening. Only something scraped along again, some noise behind the door. The dead broad wasn't opening the door, was she?

"Good God!" He tore down the road he had come, and when he was already behind the hedge, he heard the door of the van creak rustily.

He ran into the casualty ward frightened, and banged into the white-painted doorframe. The orderly was swearing listlessly at the man on duty. They had been swearing at each other for some time and, sprawled on a chair, the orderly was finishing a cigarette.

"Hey, it seems the old woman, uh–revived." Fomka whistled and collapsed on the chair next to the orderly.

"Go on," the orderly waved him away.

The doctor on duty looked thoughtfully at them and said, amused, "You send your workers out after a live woman—they drag her back dead, you're about to put her in the morgue—and it turns out she's alive." The doctor's glasses flashed like fire. "Here's what, drag her over. Right over here." He pointed at the poorly-washed tile floor. "Dead or alive. Slobs!"

"Take it easy," the orderly frowned. Throwing his cigarette on the floor, right where the old woman was supposed to lie, he went outside. Fomka was hardly able to get up and moved warily behind.

The orderly strode boldly down the road, cussing between his teeth, his white coat flapping. But when he neared the hedge behind which the truck was parked, he slowed down.

"Listen, did you open the door?" he asked in a whisper for some reason, peering through the hedge.

"Nah-me," Fomka gasped out in a single breath. He froze to the spot in terror.

"Come on." The orderly grabbed his arm in his huge palm, and they both quietly stepped out from behind the hedge.

The door of the van was wide open, just like the door to the morgue, and the thick stench of dead bodies reached them outside. There was no one there. The old woman had disappeared. The scratched iron floor rippled, empty.

* * *

"Listen, and stop quivering." The orderly shook Fomka, who was numb with cold. "Maybe the watchman took her into the basement?"

"Hey!" he yelled into the darkness. And again the sounds rumbled, rushed down, until they echoed somewhere very far away, divided up and died away. But one high, thin voice—someone's—still yelled a long and dreadful "hey!"

"Let's go." The orderly went down.

"Y-you go." Fomka stood up to him firmly this time and waited by the truck.

"Dirty clod!" The orderly was grumbling somewhere in the darkness already. Then he said something else, but Fomka did not understand what—his ears were clogged with fear. He spent another five minutes or so in torment and even stole up to the cabin, wondering if he should not cut out, when there, down below, someone let out a frightened scream.

"That does it," Fomka decided. He ran over to the truck and grabbed the door handle, but in his terror he jerked it up. He burst into the cabin, whimpering in impatience.

Fomka was already in the cabin and turning the key in the ignition rapidly, when the pale, dishevelled watchman emerged from the darkness of the morgue with his shirt torn open, and behind him, the orderly with his face a pale gray...

\* \* \*

A dark rumor jolted through the city and rustled, bent in everyone's teeth. Corpses were running away from the morgue. Everyone there had run away, young and old. The morgue was empty, and the watchman nearly murdered. They can turn up anywhere. You talk for a whole hour at the bus stop with the old accountant from the department next door, and at work you find out that he died over a week ago. Consequently, you were speaking with a corpse. In the store, the tanned girl behind you in line can very easily turn out to be dead. There were all sorts of things like that going on. The wife of a certain prominent administrator was crushed to death by a bus that day, which her husband, naturally did not even suspect. He found her at her housework, and could scarcely suppose that his wife's head, which she had wrapped in a terrycloth towel "because of a migraine," was completely squashed in five places. At night, when the successful husband, exhausted from his day's labors, went to sleep, his wife gnawed through his throat, and they ran away together from their beautiful three-room apartment, which the executive committee had only recently assigned them.

The nearly-murdered watchman was sitting all this time in a beerhall, and for a mug he would share his experience with all comers.

"Were you scared, Pops?" the citizens wanted to know, forgetting to blow off the foam, so it fizzed and ran down the mugs, grimy from dirty fingers.

"Of course I wasn't scared, my boy," the watchman answered pensively, turning to some individual and slurping the yellow dregs. They got him beer out of turn, and he was respectably drunk. His shirt, mended in front, was all covered with spots. His wizened beard, fluffed out in the sun, was spattered with beer, and shining roach scales gleamed in it like mica.[2]

"Of course not. I've been sitting in the basement lately," the watchman continued. "I was going to listen to the radio a bit, hear what they had to say about the weather. And just as I was reaching out my hand, someone goes and grabs it..."

The line fidgeted and curled round the corner, tried to get closer to the old man. But he did not like that. He swore at them to stop getting dust in his mug, and took the box he was sitting on and moved away a little. Many people just gave up on the line and followed the old guy.

"... I look—God! The fellow that's got me by the arm is the one that threw himself off the roof three days ago. The corpse gets up from the shelf, eyes closed, lays ahold of me and says, 'No you don't, pops, you'll disturb us with your music. We feel awful enough as it is.' And then he slams that radio over my head."

Someone gasped, someone ran for another mug, everyone felt sorry for the old guy.

"See, gave me a lump." The old man showed the crown of his head, on which a huge violet bump appeared through his thin hair.

"That's how it was, my boy..."

\* \* \*

Marusia did not know anything about this—she was waiting for the Evil One. She was scared for her mother and she feared for her father. With difficulty, she prevailed on them to visit some relatives. She was left alone in the house. But when the Evil One comes, what then?

As usual, the policeman was standing at the crossing, battling the cars. He was pale, alert. He did not look at Marusia; he looked at the cars, battled the cars.

Marusia opened the window. If something happens, she will scream. The patrolman will hear and help her. How could he not help? He will save Marusia from the Evil One. Only will he be able to? The pendulum ticked in its dark case on the wall, and it got even darker.

A door quivered, a distant door. On the stairs the steps bent, creaked, and Marusia sensed someone in the entryway already. She was so scared she could not even scream—she just moved back toward the window. Another moment and she would throw herself down on the black asphalt.

The locked door, with all its bolts drawn, creaked and opened wide, opened like a door to the grave, empty.

Marusia wanted to scream. She looked with a hard, fixed eye through the window. The patrolman was standing right nearby, outside the window, looking at her, grinning with his broad canines.

"I've come, Marusia, as I promised."

"Only tell me, Marusia." He was not by the window, he spoke behind her back. She turned—he was standing in the room, grinning with his broad canines. "Tell me, were you in the church last night?"

"No." She trembled.

"Did you see what I was doing there?"

"No."

"No?" The Evil One clasped her in scorching arms. She could not scream, nor tear herself away, and he fastened on her lips with a kiss. Her lips were cut as if by a knife, and the cold of his teeth sank into her heart. The Evil One tore her body, destroyed her soul.

Marusia had nearly perished when the darkness before her eyes opened and a little old woman appeared in the light and whispered something. Marusia jerked back and screamed, "Dmitry!"

"What?" The Evil One recoiled, ground his teeth, spun round. "Well, then, tomorrow your father will die!"

And he disappeared.

\* \* \*

Marusia awoke. It was evening over the city, and evening in her eyes. Rain stretched over the roofs. Wet, they stooped.

Drops came through the open window, rapped on the windowsill, shattered, and sprayed into the room. Like a wet, black cross, the asphalt lay before the house. There was no patrolman, no car. Quiet. Only the raindrops tapping.

She got up and could barely take a step. She glanced in the dim mirror with its dusty crack and broken edge, and she did not recognize herself. Bloody lips, her face badly bitten, and terrifying eyes. What had happened to her? Was that how she looked? She had no strength left, her heart was scarcely beating.

She washed up. Blood from her lips mixed with the pinkening water and ran off. Her swollen lips hurt, and her body hurt. Her hands were black and blue. She sensed that far beyond the rain, beyond the wind and the raindrops, a ringing had begun. It was not a lot of bells that rang, but one. So quiet, sad, it strikes. And a light chime scales off the weatherbeaten bellmetal, slips over the earth like a shadow, and flies into the city, whirls over the houses. And the rain raps against it, brings it down in raindrops until it is completely soaked, heavy with rain. It breaks with a raindrop through Marusia's window. Then it dies away.

And Marusia heard life dying away inside her. She guessed where the bells were ringing, and her heart stood quite still. They are ringing in the church where she was last night. They're ringing for her father, who will die tomorrow.

## CHAPTER FIVE

Borka ambled down the street, counting windows in the buildings. There were few windows in the gray walls, and the ones there were, were like dark crevices—people swarmed in them. The whole city swarmed in them. And Borka had lived in one, dirty, dark, until they evicted him. Where now?

He tried to see Efim. After all, he was his friend, his buddy. Yeah, right! Efim had turned his back on him. It turned out he was no friend at all. How could you be a friend anyway, when not people, but apartments, were precious here. What are people, what good are they? You get married or write denunciations for a residence permit. You kill for an apartment.

Borka had a residence permit. He was lucky—he worked at the factory. He had money, and a roof over his head. What more do you need? And he did not live in some dormitory, either—he had a room. His own room. He could get married, bring his wife in. And they would have registered his wife, and he could have had a family. When a child was born, they would have been put on the waiting list at the executive committee. Really, his room was not very big—nine meters—they just might have put them on that list. And then... Borka did not even think about it, and about how wonderful it would have been.

He liked girls. Not just one—he liked many of them, but Marusia more than the others. She is beautiful—what more can you say? But then *he* turned up, in his red shirt, and Borka was left with nothing. And now they have taken away his apartment because he was fired.

Tell someone about it—they will not believe it. Seven years he worked at the factory, seven years he fulfilled the norm. And you do not just fulfill it, you have to overfulfill it,[1] and that is just what he did. He earned both the residence permit and the apartment honestly. He had already started saving for furniture, and suddenly everything was lost.

Tell someone about it—they will laugh they will not believe it. But here is Borka, without work, without an apartment. Seven years, and he was not late to his station once. And all because he refused to go out in the country and help get in the potato harvest.[2]

"I don't imagine anyone's coming from the kolkhoz to help with my work," he reasoned, and laughed. He did not go when the others did.

For a month he worked as before. For a month his factory brigade broke their backs in the fields in the rain. They tore the harvest from the earth with shovels, and some with rakes—there were not enough shovels to go around—then they scraped the mud off the tubers with their hands, and put them in sacks. Enormous sacks, knolls of gray sackcloth on the black, wet earth. But who is going to come for them if there is no road, if a truck all covered with mud barely crawls through the village, and beyond the village would completely vanish in the mud, disappear into the earth? So they dragged the sacks to the village.

They came back from the kolkhoz angry, but the city seemed heaven to them. And long after, Borka noticed, their faces broke into smiles as they walked around the city. The asphalt beneath their feet made them happy, the brick houses, and the kolbasa[3] in the store. They stopped looking at Borka, despised him for his "treachery." As if they had been rounded up and put into prison, heaven knows what for, while Borka the informer was still at large. How could they forgive that?

The foreman disliked him more than the others, though he did not go anywhere either. So Borka's work was going worse—complicated stuff that did not pay much. That is up to the foreman.

Borka was harrassed for a long time. He could not stand it, and went to the factory committee seeking justice. And he found that he had been sacked, left without a residence permit. He was finished.

Down the street Borka ambled, counting the windows in the buildings. There were few windows in the gray walls, and the ones there were, were like dark crevices—people swarmed in them. But there was nowhere to live—it is enough to make you put a razor to your throat.

Borka went out of the city. He came out onto a path. Where will it take him? Borka walks on. To the left—a ravine, noisy and dark in the wind's breath. The bushes' damp shadows tremble in it. Beyond the ravine, far below, roofs shine beneath the sun, gardens bristle with motionless twigs. To the right—a meadow, like a cap of green fur, faded in the hot sun.

The earthen path turned its body back, the slope and ravine moved off, and the meadow disappeared behind the bushes. A church appeared. White, it shines in the sun. A gold cross blazes in the sky, glitters.

He went up to the church. The doors were locked, and there were no people around. Just an old woman on the porch, on the warm, worn stone. Small, a bundle of rags, ordinary—only her glance was strange.

"Hi, granny!" he said, and only then noticed how quiet it was all around. The birds were silent, turned to leaves; the dragonfly did not rustle his fine, mica wings;

the grasshopper was not chirring, like a leaf himself, on long, mechanical legs. There was none of the sound that day makes at daytime. It was quiet as night, all around.

The old woman smiled to the hollows of her pitted gums.

"Hello, sonny. Why so sad?"

"What's to be happy about, granny? They kicked me out of my job, and I've got nowhere to live—just woe."

"Woe? No, son, that's not woe yet," the old woman smiled. "Woe will be later, when I come to you. But you came yourself, paid me a visit. What kind of woe is that? Since you got here on your own, you'll manage to find your way back, and Woe will not hold you."

"So you are Woe, grandma?"

"Woe, sonny, Woe, but don't you be afraid, it wasn't me—people made me like that."

The old woman looked at the sorrow-stricken Borka and smiled again. "Stop grieving. Listen to what I have to say..."

The wind rushed and whipped the grass, slammed hard into Borka and caught his hair. Shadows lumbered, closed in, and in an instant, the church bowed and disappeared with the bells, the old woman, and the porch... High in the sky the meadow flew like a cap.

\* \* \*

Borka saw himself in a dark apartment, where the smell of fish and frying fat stuck to the walls. Where the floor bent, creaked beneath his feet, and where, in the crevices stuffed with greasy dirt, cockroach feelers quivered. Behind the rags of old wallpaper they tinkled long on iron strings and clapped solidly, as on a suitcase. A drunken, phlegm-filled voice broke out:

> I've been cheated,
> Been mistreated,
> Lost my heart to you...

A second voice—a woman's—laughed, said, "Come on," and gave something a smacking kiss.

"What do you mean, 'come on?'" gurgled the first, breaking off his song. "You're a bitch, Duska."

"Come, come," the broad's voice was not angry. "Don't start a row, you gay dog in blue," and the voice laughed long again.

> I've been cheated,
> Been mistreated,
> Lost my heart to you...

Something creaked—the cockroach feelers took cover—and a woman passed down the hall to the kitchen, pressing her hands against her washed-out housecoat, darned all over, and fearfully bowing her head in its white kerchief. She sighed, muttered something, and when she took the lid off the saucepan on the stove, her pale old face shuddered. In the saucepan, in the thin soup with a few leaves of cabbage, floated a mouse.

Her weak eyes dimmed with tears, and she cried. Bent over, she went to her room. Why? She was sick, she bought a head of cabbage with the last of her money, she could hardly stand, she fixed some soup. She thought she would eat a little something hot—maybe it would get better... And they put a mouse in it...

Heavy tears broke free and fell. But she did not get

to her room. The iron string clanged one last time, and the neighbors' door, covered with torn oilcloth, creaked and swung open.

"Ah, the old lady's out for a walk." Out stepped a woman with a boozy face. Her dress was unbuttoned, and her meaty breasts heaved against the buttons. "When are you going to clean the apartment,[4] you old witch? Or do I have to do it for you?"

"Grisha," she called into the alcoholic darkness. Artishchev, distorted with drunkenness, came out with a dark blue T-shirt on his hairy body and sky-blue military riding breeches.

"There she is, the old jade! See, she won't clean, and she messed up the whole apartment."

"I'm sick," she answered, and pressed her hands to her dry, sunken mouth.

"Sick?" Artishchev screwed up his eyes. "You're a fool, granny. If you're sick, you should go to an old folks' home. But you hang onto an apartment, don't let people live. And to think that people make a fuss over you..." He banged on the guitar and bared the teeth in his dark face. The woman yawned with her smeary trap, went out to the kitchen and lifted the saucepan lid.

"Oh look, now mice are crawling into her saucepans!" She laughed, bent double, smacking herself wetly on the thighs.

A sob nudged the old woman's tears. She rushed towards her door, but Artishchev did not let her pass. He stood there, rocking from his heels to his toes, blocking her way.

"Don't run away, granny, you won't escape from the police...," he said seriously. Both eyes were crossed from drink. "I'll speak openly: if you don't move by yourself, I'll evict you, just watch..." He grabbed her by the shoulder, shook her and clenched his other hand in a fist, dark, tobacco-stained, with bulging veins.

Nearly unconscious, she locked herself in her room. She had no more strength. Tears oppressed her. She fell on the bed, covered with a bedspread with a shepherd and shepherdess on it—a present from her husband. She grew quiet.

Someone struck the door with his fist.

"Watch it, granny. Remember what I said."

> I've been cheated,
> Been mistreated...

Borka sat on a stool in the kitchen and pondered. He looked out the window, dull from dust and water spots. He looked closely at the pieces of sea between the houses, and at the white houses made of shellrock. He even made out one sign, apparently *Kerchen City Executive Committee.* But maybe it was something else, who knows. He stood up, so the city outside the window and the sea pitched downward into the dust. Going up to the stove, he took off the saucepan and poured the soup into the slop pail along with the mouse.

The woman and Artishchev were not there, only the cockroaches rustling, stirring in the crevices. Borka sliced himself some black bread, sprinkled it with damp salt and chewed it up, taking large swallows. He did not touch anything else.

Pieces of the broken sea pounded outside the window. The pieces rolled.

Somewhere near, right beneath the walls—drunken voices. Someone's soles shuffled, knocking stones loose.

\* \* \*

"On the Black Sea shooore..." The woman appeared, quite drunk by now, with two obscene-looking fellows. She reeled down the hall, nearly knocking down Borka, who was looking out from the kitchen.

Blackest sea you'll ever see...

They burst into the room, clinked glasses, and poured, hardly waiting before they started playing around.

In the morning the fellows went past the neighbor's door into the twilight, which had just begun to lift. They were swearing—the woman did not see them out—they were angry about something. One staggered and stopped, leaning his back against the wall. He struck a match on a box and lit up.

"There she is, the whore." He looked at the neighbor's door—the broad had told them about her. "You old varmint!" He kicked his heel against the whitewashed plywood. "Come out of there, bitch..."

"Cut it out," the second quieted him. "To hell with her, let's go."

"No, wait a minute." And he hit the door with his heel again as he passed.

They went out... There were a lot of people on the street.

\* \* \*

She wrote the complaint with difficulty, laboriously. She cried, begged them to protect her. For she had no one to protect her—both husband and son had died at the front, and she is an invalid—help! But who will help if she has no strength left? Her neighbors on the street felt sorry for her, but who is going to argue with the police? Who will stand up to them?

They called her down to the station. She did not know what to do. She went. And Borka followed her. It is a good thing he was invisible.

"Why are you slandering our employees?" they asked. "You write libelous complaints to all the review boards, disgracing the name of honest citizens. You think you can get away with that?"

She just stood there. She did not know what to say, not the first word.

"Not a chance. We're warning you: if it happens again, we'll make you answer for it."

They spoke so politely.

"But why?" was all she said. She knew she was saying the wrong thing. Borka knew too, and rushed in to argue, to testify. A lot of good that did! They did not see him and did not hear, although there he was, right there in front of them. So they went out with nothing.

At home, the neighbor said, "Well, now what, dropped downtown, you old jade? Get anything out of them? Here they are, those complaints of yours." She took the crumpled letters and started tearing them up. "See, see, you shit."

Artishchev laughed through his teeth in the darkness, a cockade stuck up from his cap.

\* \* \*

She cried. Who would protect her, if she has no strength left? Is she supposed to protect herself, or what?

In the morning, only the woman went out, closed the door, locked the bolt. Now watch her bring some guys home. She was trembling all over. Even when they swore at her through the wall at night, threatened to kill her, the hammering in her throat, the tearing inside, was not like this. She waits, what will happen? She locked herself in her room. She was afraid to go out to the kitchen, so Borka just sat there. He was worried too. The lamp smoked dimly beneath the ceiling. The city stood in the windows. They waited.

\* \* \*

Something crashed on the stairway. An iron key turned in the keyhole. It stopped, then started jiggling again. Borka's heart leapt.

Someone threw all his weight against the door.

"Hey, you, open up."

The neighbor woman's voice yelled. A second, deep, spoke briefly nearby, and when it had finished, was lost behind the door.

"Open up, I say!" The cracked boards trembled. Dust fell out of the crevices. Stingy bitch!"

Someone stamped his feet all the way through the entryway and tramped heavily down the steps.

"Wait, where are you going?" the woman yelled. "Just wait a minute..."

Down below the fellow swore in a booming voice that carried up the whole stairway, swore hoarsely through the attic, and struck the outer door.

"Hell with you, you shit..." They started knocking again, and the voice in the corridor rushed up and down.

She lay on the bed, locked in her room. The bedspread was bunched up under her and it quivered—she was trembling all over. And she was not glad she had not let the woman in just now. The alarm clock ticked on the dull, doily-covered top of the bureau. What could happen?

Suddenly something flashed in the window, and broke out a star of glass. Shards rained down, ringing on the floor where the stone rolled, rumbled.

"Hey, shit, now you'll answer for it all!" The neighbor's voice carried up from below, outside the window now. "You'll never forget this..."

\* \* \*

The next day, someone knocked at the apartment door. The bolt on the door was open, and they could just walk in. She heard them come down the hall—the neighbor woman, she thought. But when they knocked at her door, she knew it was someone else. A polite, persistent knock.

"Who's there?" she asked, and was already opening the door herself.

"Sanitary service, to extermine cockroaches."

"Just a minute, just a minute." She opened the door. It was dark in the hall, and two white smocks hung empty, like shrouds. Medical orderlies. Both strong guys. At first she could not figure it out, though she was seized with alarm. But when she jumped aside, it was too late—they grabbed her.

"H-e-l-p!" she screamed, as if they were killing her. But who would help?

Only Borka rushed about in the darkness. But what could he do? They did not see him and did not hear.

They led her out to the street, the heavy door creaked, rattled, and they drove the madwoman to the madhouse. But what sort of madwoman was she?

* * *

As it happened—and it rarely does—they released her. And they did not hold her long—three days. They did not really harrass her much, either. "Nervous exhaustion," the doctor concluded. "Needs rest." And the others agreed with him. "But the patient in question is of sound mind," he elaborated, and the others did not argue. They did not even find signs of schizophrenia, which was quite surprising.

They released her and even gave her a certificate saying she was normal, so she would not be brought in again. So it happened, and it rarely does. But she did not understand. She had very little time left before she really would go nuts.

She got home on foot all the way across town. She went to her apartment. The lock on the door was jimmied, and the plywood broken through.

"What is this?" Everything in the room was turned upside down, all her things jumbled up, scattered. The bedspread with the shepherd and shepherdess was missing—a present from her husband—and the little vase of green glass was smashed. The shards looked up from the floor.

"But why..." She started gathering up the shards, as if she could really glue it back together.

Borka stood in the hall and looked at her. There was something pressing, some sharp pain in his chest.

The neighbor woman rushed down the hall, right through Borka. For just an instant he could not breathe. She strode straight into the room.

"Ah, you old jade, so they released you. Well, it

doesn't matter, you'll clear out of here now, you've been evicted, you old whore!"

She grew faint and did not even hear what was said to her, she was that frightened.

"Gather your junk and move on out. You don't live here any more. Hear what I said?"

"You have no right!" Her lips spoke of their own accord. "Who gave you the right to insult an old woman?"

"What? Say that again," the woman yelled, her face distorted. She shoved her in the chest. "Say it."

She could not keep her balance. Her foot caught on something. She fell. She did not have the strength to get up. She cried quietly, a senile, turbid flood.

Wail on, you shit, you'll find out."

\* \* \*

She lay there until evening. A few times she disappeared and floated quietly and softly in the dense black. She would turn up again on the floor, amid her scattered things.

The setting sun scorched flame and fire through the window. It hung angrily just over the earth. The glass grew bent, bloody, as it threw out pieces of reflections—the floor, the drawer of the bureau—and fell on the gray walls. The pane broken by the rock coldly rolled its dreadful, ulcered eye.

At night a breeze started blowing. She came to, got up. She walked around the room, stumbling over her jumbled things, crunching and ringing on the broken glass. She went up to the door, hooked it and blocked it with the dark weight of the bureau. Where did she find the strength? She shrank all over and froze beside it. She sat there until morning.

She did not move, did not budge, when, as she expected, they pounded on the door.

"Open up, granny, police," they yelled in thick voices behind the door. Artishchev and others were yelling.

She sat there, did not budge. They kicked the door hard with their boots.

"Agh, you old shit!" Artishchev was surprised. "Resisting authority?" He started ramming, pounding the door. The din rose with the dust through the whole house. The door bent, cracked in that din. It held, though the hook bent.

"Force the door to open out," Artishchev commanded. "One, two..." Something cracked slowly, slowly in the boards, and then snapped, fell. Curses flew through the apartment. They had broken the door handle. Now they could not open it at all.

It quieted down behind the door. Artishchev was the last to swear, sputter something. A motorcycle roared, gunning outside the window, and it could be heard for a long time as it raced through the city. It vanished and reappeared, gunning even louder...

Suddenly it grew dark. Artishchev sprang up in the window. He was faded, distorted by the glass, except for a bright button where the pane was broken. His military cap rose above the city, and shut out half the city and the sea with its red band.

"You're resisting authority," he wheezed, grabbing the frame and smashing the glass with his boot. "So..."

Another head in a cap appeared, and another... Artishchev had already climbed into the room He restrained himself, did not look at the old woman. He went up to the trunk and started hurling every last thing in it out the window.

The two others climbed in, started helping him. They threw the bureau away from the door and opened it wide.

Artishchev threw the trunk over, but when he had gathered the things in a heap and stepped over to the window, she just could not stand it.

"Bandit! What are you doing!" She threw herself at him, and seized the old dresses and her husband's suit, which he had never put on. She bought it for him herself. She had wanted to give him a present. But she never had—she only cried over it at night.

"Lousy scum," he said brutishly and, without letting go of the heap, swung round and struck her with his whole body... The walls and ceiling broke loose. She found herself on the floor, dark blood on her lips. He had hit her in the face with his shoulder.

"So much for her, the pest," the other two laughed.

Artishchev no longer walked; he rushed about the room, throwing things out the window. They scattered in the wind.

"Well, why are you pottering around over here?" He ran over to the bureau and shoved aside the pottering policemen, who just could not manage to push it into the hall. "Here's how you do it!" He seized hold of the bureau and, smashing the knobs on the doorframe, shoved it out of the room. He picked up the trunk...

She got up and threw herself at him again. She wanted to seize, not her things, but that odious face of his. He saw her and hit her in the head with his fist and in the stomach with his boot. She groaned so loud and dreadfully that he started back, and the others froze, exchanged glances.

She wheezed, collapsed face down on the worn

floorboards.

"Hey!" His buddies were frightened. "Did you kill her or what?" One took off his cap and wiped his forehead with his sleeve. The other stepped into the hall.

"Now we've fucked up," Artishchev said hoarsely. "What'll we do with her?"

He went up to her and took her hand. It was warm, the artery was beating. He grinned with a wooden mouth. "She's alive, don't worry."

"What's up, my dandies?" The woman came in, her fat cheeks jouncing.

"Just look." One pointed to the old woman.

"Is that all?" She laughed. "Frightened already, you brave chaps? Don't get upset, I'll just wash her little face, the scum."

She lightly picked up the old woman and led her off to the kitchen.

\* \* \*

Out into the street, into the dust, onto the stones they carried the trunk and the bed and the scratched-up bureau. They piled the clothes on top. Artishchev got a new lock, sticky, smelling of oil. They locked and sealed the door and went away. It grew quiet in the empty, locked apartment. Only the alarm clock ticked with a flick of its second hand in the broad's room.

The cement in the wall of the empty, sealed room moved, wrinkled. Borka came out of the wall, sad and quite gray. He was choked with anger, and ashamed that he had been frightened of the police. But how could he have helped?

He walked, sort of breezed around the room. The floor was bare, just broken glass on it. And a white ribbon fluttered by the window, caught on a nail.

\* \* \*

She walked down the street in her wet dress, with her badly bruised face. She walked and did not see the cowardly faces of her neighbors, their pathetic, crooked smiles. She did not hear their quiet words, pitying themselves and her, and did not see their houses, skulking back from the street. She did not notice the city by the badly-bruised sea. She walked.

\* \* \*

The next day she bethought herself, and decided to go to the hospital. People are mean, but you have to live. She went to the hospital to show the marks of the beatings inflicted upon her. They examined her, pitied her and wrote a report right then of the black-and-blue marks, the bruises, the contusions. They wrote at length. And the doctor pitied her.

From the hospital, she went to the police station with the report, to prosecute.

"Prosecute?" the chief laughed, and his neck glowed red. He looked at her severely.

"You want a trial? I'll give you a trial. You'll answer to the government for everything."

\* \* \*

It was dark and cold in the cell. What did she need light for? She was arrested, not the criminals who tormented her. She was under guard, she was behind bars. But how could this be? Is she crazy? Is she not imagining it? No, it is all there—the bars, the cell with its slimy floor and damp walls.

In the daytime it was hot, she could hardly breathe. Her old legs grew even colder, shivered even more. No, she was not imagining it. She is being prosecuted, not them. God, what is this?

"Well, you've done your writing and complaining, you old dribbler," the guard grinned. "You managed to get up to the Central Committee. You've still got Nixon left to write to, maybe he could help," he laughed, choked with guffaws. "Or write to the UN, that would be useful too..."

She trembled, shrank all over, and refused to eat.

"She's on a hunger strike!" The guard's guffaws stuck in his throat, strangled him. "Good girl, that's a bonus in my pocket. Fool!"

They immediately stopped bringing her food. If she asked for something, they would refuse.

It was dark and cold in the cell. And in the daytime it was so hot she could hardly breathe. What did she need to breathe for? She is being prosecuted, not them. God, what is this?

She was sick. She had not eaten for nine days. She lay on the bent, splintery boards. Though it was forbidden to lie down in the daytime, they graciously permitted her to do so after she had lain on the stone floor for twenty-four hours. Now she lay contorted on the boards, racked with coughing. She was starving, but who knew about it? No one. And it is no one's business, even if she dies there. "An old woman," they will say, "she just kicked off. About time."

She was crying.

On the ninth day she was called to trial. She refused to go, and even if she had agreed, she would not have been able—her legs would not carry her. They were not disconcerted—they brought a stretcher and carried her off on it. And in court no one was surprised. Apparently, people are often carried in. Only the escorts laughed: "Keep your eyes peeled, or the old gal'l run off."

Sitting patiently through it all, the neighbor woman was there alone. Artishchev did not even come. And why should he come? They started reading. They read a lot, and mentioned everything: antisocial behavior, taunting the neighbor, the unsanitary condition of her room, refusal to obey police employees, even direct attack upon their persons... They read a lot.

Everything was spinning. The woman flew up to the ceiling, and the judges crashed down with the bench and huge chairs into the darkness beneath the window.

"Sit down." A policeman came up behind her, held her by the shoulder so she would not fall on the dock where they had carried her on the stretcher. She could not stretch out like on the stretcher. He held her firmly. She could not scream, could not tear herself away.

There were no outsiders in the courtroom, either simply because no one came, or because they did not let anyone in.

She waited for them to let her speak. They did not. They did not even ask her anything. And what should they have asked her?

"I wish to speak!" she cried, when the court rose to withdraw for deliberation.

"No one gave you leave," said one judge, turning around. He was a little younger, wearing glasses. The others had already left the courtroom, and he went out after them.

"Sit down granny, and shut your mouth." The policeman tugged at her. "Sit down quietly."

"... the Court, having considered the case of citizeness Osipova, Alexandra Konstantinovna, sentences citizeness Osipova..."

The courtroom grew black...

... and the court gave me a suspended sentence of three years. And now I have nowheres to live and nothing to live on. They don't pay me my pension now that I'm not registered, and I don't have no means of support any more. How am I to live now? I spend the night at the neighbors', but they don't always let me when they don't feel like it. I go to the railroad station, but they already know me there. The stationmaster gives orders to throw me out. My husband and son both died in the war with the Fascists and I was left all alone, an invalid myself, with nobody to protect me. What did they die for? So their wife and mother could have her little room taken away? All these years I've been afraid of the neighbor woman and lots of other evil people, but now I'm not afraid of anything. Let them really put me in jail, at least I'll have a roof over my head. At least they'll feed me, one way or another. I'll know myself that I'm suffering, but innocent. If my husband and son knew, if they could see what the goverment for which they died is doing to me! So how is this goverment better than the Fascists who were enemies? They would curse this goverment as I curse it now, not fearing nothing no more. Where are those Party members they write about in books?[5] Now I understand there ain't any—only scoundrels...

"Yes, yes," the writer could not help muttering, breaking into a sweat and running his palm over his gray head, "When does she get to the point..."

... The Fascists were our enemies, so if you killed them, it was the enemies you was killing. Our government drove me from my home, threw me to my death. Why? Because I worked forty years, became an invalid. Now the neighbor woman's got the whole apartment to herself. She got what she was after! Under our goverment, what you'll never get through honest work in your whole life you'll get fast enough by theft and murder. Yes, yes, murder. And not just of one, but two people. I know it for a fact. Earlier, my neighbor wasn't registered at all and rented a room from two old ladies, teachers. And a month later, one was knifed in the city park. Robbed, they said. But two weeks after that, the other one, her sister, drowned, though she was old and never went swimming in the sea. The whole police force knew my neighbor by then. Many of them came to see her, carried on with her. And they hushed up the affair. They say themselves she drowned her. And they gave her a room and later moved her in with me, because I was alone in the apartment, and there's a lot of space. That's not allowed, they said. I told the divisional inspector about the murders and then wrote to the regional court about them. The assistant public prosecutor promised to investigate, but he didn't and he doesn't answer my letters. They say he doesn't work there any more. Apparently he was an honest man and they put him out of the way too. Our goverment has no love for honest folk. It loves thieves and murderers...

"Well, I guess it's obvious that she's crazy," laughed the writer, relieved. "She really got carried away." The rich yellow light of the desk lamp swung across his no-longer-young face, so well know to the television audience.

In his shadow stood Borka, a different, quite gray Borka, who saw everything and suffered for everything. He had been at the trial too, and had wandered through the train station. Now he stood in the dense shadow of responsible workers, and read the letter with them. But was there only one letter like that? Hundreds, thousands of letters screamed, howled in wild voices. Every day — thousands! You could not answer them all and could not read each one through. What can you do? People, bent at office desks, scribble out formal replies, formal replies to misfortune. The letters return, rush back into the hands of those against whom the complaints were issued "for review." Misfortune rises like a wall all around...

The man straightened the lamp, and the light swung his shadow aside.

"Yes." He did not read farther, but just glanced at the end:

> ... One old man arrived in summer and stayed with us. He fought all through the war. He was a partisan, in the Fascists' prison camps twice. He came back healthy to his motherland from Germany and captivity. And they put him in prison for ten years, made a cripple of him. Our fanatics are worse than the Fascists'. Now he drinks and cries and shouts "Heil, Hitler!" under his breath. He shouts under his breath because in our country they don't let us shout anything full force except cuss words. After all they've done to me, I want to shout "Heil, Hitler!" too.
>
> cc:
> Supreme Soviet
> Central Committee
> Writers' Union

"Well, I guess it's obvious that she's crazy," the writer repeated and sighed. "I ought to put an editorial in *The Literary Gazette*.[6] We've got so many mix-ups and squabbles... Ye-e-e-s, just look what letters they write. Someone, in his haste apparently, offended this person, behaved callously, and it took its toll on her morbid imagination. I've got to write. I'll have them set her up in a hospital somewhere. She's a human being after all. For conscience sake I've got to."

And the writers' conscience, so sensitive to the people's misfortune, was soothed, and the writer went off to dine in the Oak Room of the Writers' Club.

* * *

The wind rushed and whipped the grass, slammed hard into Borka and caught his hair. Again the white church is shining in the sun. The gold cross blazes in the sky, glitters. And the old woman on the warm, worn stone, small, a bundle of rags, looks at Borka.

"Do you understand now?"

"So was that Woe, grandma?"

"No, sonny, Woe was with me, came into me. Woe is when they gnaw out your heart. You have everything. No one's deprived you of your home, your job. They only did violence to your heart, took away your heart. That's Woe. What you've seen is Misfortune!"

And Borka understood: It is not the old woman who walks through the city, pees in the railroad stations it is Misfortune! Misfortune grows, Misfortune rises like a wall all around.

# CHAPTER SIX

Her father had died. He lay pale in the coffin and shuddered when they walked through the room. When Marusia and her mother walked. No one else came, not even relatives. The high coffin was on the table, the window at its head. And the face was pale as wax on the forehead and cheeks, and black in the hollows of the eyes and the slightly open slit of the mouth.

People from the regional hospital came and certified the death. Then it was empty and quiet again, just the deceased on the table, shuddering when they walked. The newspaper lay on the sofa; there was no one to read it now. The lines of print fell in ranks.

Outside the window, dim and distant, bells pealed again in that church outside of town. All day and all night Marusia heard that peal, quiet, quite thin as if no man, but the wind, rang the black bell.

They refused to inter her father in the city. They said there was no space available. All the cemeteries were over-crowded; they had no place to put their own. And as ill-luck would have it, the deceased had no relatives buried anywhere to put him in with—in the relative's grave. There was no sense crying, begging; they had to bury him in a field, in a new cemetery, blowing with dust, sprouting crosses, where there was not a single tree and no grass —only the earth, rusty as iron.

Marusia went to the office, and they came to an agreement. He would be buried tomorrow. And she paid the money for the lot and signed where she had to, where they pointed.

She walked slowly back through the city, she did not want to go home. Though she knew that her mother was there alone and waiting for her, she just could not force herself—she dropped in on her girlfriends.

"Maruska, how great you came by," Irina greeted her, smiling and, it seemed, looking at her with a certain annoyance from under a lock of fair hair that had fallen in her face. "We've got a whole group here carousing..."

She wanted to leave immediately, but felt awkward. She just managed a smile and followed Irina, svelte, tall in spike heels.

"Welcome my friend!" Irina shouted.

She went in—and the lights went out, streamed, poured on the floor from the dim lamp in the corner and from two candles in a brass candlestick. Among the young men and girls sat the Evil One. His shirt blazed with hellish fire, and the cards in his hand rustled, flew snapping from palm to palm.

"Hello, Marusia." He bared his teeth, flashed his thick canines. "I'm doing magic tricks, watch..."

And the cards snapped, flew faster and froze in one hand, huddled in a pack.

"Draw one." And he held out the pack to Marusia, grinning slightly.

She did not remember how she took the card. She turned it up, and froze. Her hand trembled, and the card fell, spun, slipped through the air, flew straight into the Evil One's pack. Her father was on that card, he lay pale in his coffin.

"Did I guess right?" And he laughed.

"Guess what?" Irina asked, looking tenderly

at the Evil One. A handsome, cheerful fellow, how could she help but look? And she straightened the lock of hair, smoothed her skirt on her wide thighs.

"She knows what," he grinned, looking at Irina. She was overcome and did not listen to what he answered. She looked tenderly at the Evil One, yielded to him completely.

"Tell my fortune too..."

"Sure, just let me have a word with your friend, we have some business.

He took Marusia by the arm, turned away from the offended Irina, took her aside and picked up the pack again.

"Were you in the church that night?"

"No."

"Did you see what I was doing there?"

"No!" she could scarcely speak.

"Well, then you'll see another trick." And he gave her a card. "You wanted it..."

She looked—her mother was on the card lying in a coffin. But she was not pale—her face was black. Marusia could not look any longer, she burned all over, staggered, covered her eyes...

A woman appeared out of the darkness, bent down and spoke to her through bloody lips.

"Ar-ti-shchev!" repeated Marusia and uncovered her eyes.

"What?" The Evil One recoiled. Both candles went out, tracing patterns of smoke in the darkness, and the Evil One disappeared...

"Where is he?" Irina ran over. She asked so loudly that Efim stopped telling his skinny lover something, half-rose, and fumbled in his pockets, looking for a match.

"He left," was all Marusia answered and walked towards the door herself.

"You... you chased away a guy like that," she hissed angrily. "Don't come around here anymore ... fool."

The door slammed, rattling the chain on the iron locks.

\* \* \*

She walked towards home. She did not want to go, although she knew that her mother was there alone and waiting for her. But however slowly she walked, the house disentangled itself from the oblique lanes and streets, disentangled itself from the city and moved toward her with its gray corner on the crossing, with its chimney and rusty antenna, with her dead father, the window at his head.

And when she had come quite near the house, she ran into Borka. He was standing under a wet lamppost, as if under a tree, and like the house, it seemed, coming towards her with the lamppost and the road.

She looked and did not recognize him immediately. She just thought, "Borka?"

"It's me, Marusia," Borka said, quite gray. Fear disfigured his eyes like a knife.

"What's wrong, Borya?" She touched his hand— cold as the lamppost beneath which he stood.

"I've seen a lot, Marusia. Before, I'd only heard, We all heard, and sometimes, we'd even tell how... But now I've seen..." And he stopped, swallowed the pent-up words.

"My father died."

"From what?" That is what he asked, but he was thinking of something else.

"Who knows. The doctors came later, they say it was his heart." And she set off faster towards the house—she had remembered her mother, become anxious. And Borka followed.

\* \* \*

They went up the stairs, rang. It was quiet behind the door, nothing creaked, moved. It was so quiet that if a drop fell from the faucet in the kitchen, it seemed to Marusia that she would hear it.

"Where'd she go?" She hurriedly tore open her bag and, crumpling the papers she had taken to the bureau, took out her keys, started unlocking the door. She opened it, and opened the second door into the room...

Her mother was hanging dead by a rope.

It was dark in the room. The black air clotted, and the dark body seemed frozen in that air. It did not swing, did not tremble. Only the black crack of the rope stuck in the black, frozen air, sliced the room and entered her mother's body...

\* \* \*

Two corpses in the house. Two coffins lay side by side. When they were alive, her father called her mother "little one." But in death they were equal. Two identical coffins lay there. Only her father's face was white, and her mother's black, with black, swollen lips. And her mother had more flowers.

The doors were wide open, and people went in

and out. More and more old women. Rumpled, all in black kerchiefs and shapeless skirts. The ones standing by the coffin wail, keen loudly, without calling the deceased by name. They just wail, call her mother "dearest." The others stand silent, pressing the ends of their kerchiefs to their eyes. One sighs. And the ones behind them, they just talk, whisper among themselves.

They wail a bit, then step back and others wail, the ones who had been standing behind, whispering. And each one laid down a flower, sometimes a live one, but more often a paper one. Lots of flowers, and all paper. They made it depressing and dreary.

And Borka sat there, in the far corner, looking at the old women's backs. Fear racked him, disfigured his eyes and face. It seemed to Borka that they would drive him into a coffin too, strew him with paper flowers heavier than earth, and wail over him. They would gnaw out his heart, make him wander through railroad stations, and drive him into a coffin again, strew him with paper flowers heavier than earth and wail, wail over him until Judgement Day.

"Lord," Borka whispered, "just to sit quietly, so they don't notice, and be silent, silent forever. Let them do what they want with whomever they want. Just to sit quietly..."

Two policemen came in, hesitated, took off their caps, and pressed through to the corpses.

"Mm-hm... we're going to conduct an investigation," said one. "Looks like premeditated murder... for the room."

"Of course, living space is the most important thing," said the second quietly, his eyes on Marusia, who stood pale, dry-eyed in the dark crowd of old women. "She could have killed them, she had plenty of chances."

"And that one was in on it." They remembered Borka and started looking for him. "They made a deal."

They were just about to find him.

"Borya," he heard Marusia's voice, "what's wrong?"

He opened his eyes, Marusia bent over him. The corpses were there in the house, and the old women wailed, but the police were gone.

"You're suffocating, go out on the street. Stand there for a while."

"Yes, yes," he agreed. He rose on weak legs and walked towards the door. Run away from here as soon as possible. He did not look at Marusia, whom he'd once loved.

"Borya, Borya..." Marusia whispered, and her tears flowed. The old women in the house wailed, wailed...

Borka had scarcely gone out on the street and stepped onto the black asphalt when two men in civilian clothes came up to him.

"Come along with us," said one. He kept his hand in his pocket, while the second shoved a half-covered badge in Borka's face. Borka did not see anything, only a skinny tie with a glass pin in the middle, the kind the gypsies sell on the street. "He probably swiped it from a gypsy," he thought for some reason and went off with them, quaking with fear.

The others were sitting in the car.

"Take him back," said the one with the tie and turned away from Borka. He had done his job, what did he need Borka for? They drove away.

\* \* \*

They interrogated Borka and ordered him to admit that he had murdered the old couple.

"We know you didn't do it alone," the investigator persuaded him calmly, almost tenderly, "but with the daughter of the victims. She put you up to it, right?"

Borka was silent and wanted to speak. He could not. Fear deprived him of speech.

"Well, then, how did it happen?" He motioned to the escort, who came up from behind and hit Borka. He did not hit hard, but as if by accident, without noticing that he was hitting him. And Borka grew all hard with fear and did not feel pain. He waited for a second blow—feared a second blow.

"You're a weak person, morally and politically unstable, hankering after more living-space." The investigator came round the desk, stood in front of Borka. "I remember you didn't go to the kolkhoz when you were supposed to either, refused to gather potatoes, right?" He looked at him, almost sympathetically, it seemed. "But I bet you like to gobble up those potatoes, ha?" And deep in thought, without a glance at Borka, he hit him with the heel of his hand across the nose.

"So it turns out that others are supposed to work for you, which means you're going to sit like a drone on society's neck. Do you know how we handle drones?"

And suddenly Borka started trembling, a burning fear flooded through him. Borka understood that they would not forgive him the kolkhoz. *That* they would never forgive. What about the murder? They'd execute him and use the murder as a cover.

"And you're a murderer on top of it. Now you'll pay for it, all at once. Oh, how you'll pay."

And Borka understood that he was done for— done for, and he had not even noticed how it happened —and that his life was finished, cut short suddenly, at one stroke. They tied him up with rope, and threw him on the floor. They made him crawl like a gray worm, wriggling and banging on the floor boards with his knees. Borka saw that he no longer existed—fear alone wriggled on the floor. In a moment it would fly out of the window, rise above the city. There was no strength in the city, and there were no feelings left. Only three powers, three feelings. Everything was composed of them: Woe, Fear and Misfortune!

\* \* \*

In turn, one after the other, they carried out two coffins. The old women shuffled behind them. Lots of people came. They stood and walked behind the coffins. What else was there to do in the city? Just bury someone or watch others bury theirs. So they walked, lots of people.

Four slightly sauced dockers from the store, who had undertaken to carry the coprses out and lower them into the grave for a quarter century, cussed, jostled each other over the unaccustomed work, carried the coffins unevenly. The rented truck was parked some distance away. The old women had told the chauffer to drive off, and the sweaty dockers, cursing him through their teeth, carried the coffins the one block and quickly shoved them into the rickety, rattling van with a blackish-red drape on one side.

The grannies had their way—even without a band it turned out stately, like a general's funeral.

The crowd encircled the truck and helped the old ladies in. And they, accustomed to the routine, smartly took their seats around the outside on the dusty benches. They seated Marusia and crowded together to make room for the four slightly sauced dockers who'd undertaken to carry the corpses out and lower them into the grave for a quarter century.

\* \* \*

Only in the evening, when everything was over and she was home, did Marusia come to herself. Dully, without emotion, she remembered how they had strewn her parents with earth, thrown flowers down from above, some live, but mostly paper ones, and how the old women had keened with wide, old women's mouths, loudly. Marusia was probably the only one who did not hear.

She remembered Borka and was surprised. Where had he disappeared to? Had something happened? She was surprised, not worried. She was tired of that already, and tired of being afraid of everything. She knew she had not long to live herself. And why live? Why be afraid of everything?

She cleaned up the room and washed the floor. It was as before. Her father would come in a moment and lie down on the sofa, and her mother would be tracing patterns by the lamp. And in the usual way the lamp would be shaded with a newspaper so the light would not disturb her father.

She took the black rag off the mirror, folded it and threw it on a chair . She looked in the mirror.

It seemed to her that after all this she would not have a face, and should not have one. She was surprised. There was a face there, a pretty face looked at her from the mirror, cancelled by the dusty crack in the glass. She only paled, and her eyes grew quite black. She ran her palm over her face, the tender skin quivered. For the first time in all this while she nearly burst into sobs. She held back her tears.

She turned away and went to her corner, behind the partition all pasted over with photographs. She knew she would not fall asleep, but she turned off the light and climbed into bed. Perhaps she would doze off.

Night. Marusia lay and looked at the ceiling. The darkness, which had fallen heavily into the room with a flick of the switch, started to weaken. It hung just above the floor, which it had crushed down upon like a solid block a while ago, bumping into the walls and ceiling. Light now, it started stretching through the window, oozing unnoticed into the street. And the street's night wind snatched it, rushed with it through the hushed city. The city sleeps light, like an animal.

It got light in the room. Marusia looked at the ceiling behind the blue screen and remembered her family. Those who are spending the night in the earth today. The first night in the earth is hard, probably.

The sky grew dull behind the blue screen. Marusia held back her tears and remembered her family. She remembered them without emotion. She knew that she would die soon too, perhaps this very night.

\* \* \*

The daughter of the deceased, Marusia, of whom the whole house was talking, was found dead the morning after the funeral. Found quickly, and to some surprise.

Old lady Romanikha dropped in on the orphaned girl to find out how she was doing there, all by herself. She wanted to comfort her and, at the same time, ask for a ruble or two. She had to go to the store and she had no money. So she dropped in. She knocked on the door—no one answered. But where could the orphan have gone? It was still early. She pushed the door—it was not locked. What should she do? She paused and went in.

"Marusia, are you asleep?... must be." She peeped into Marusia's corner and screamed loud enough to be heard all over the house. She nearly died herself. And she—she was so young...

Marusia lay on the bed in a badly torn night dress. Her eyes looked long and madly at Romanikha. Her mouth—an open wound—was clotted with blood, and one cheek was bitten through. Her teeth shone. And Marusia's body was stripped, stiffened, twisted in its death throes, torn with deep wounds. With ulcered wounds the body lay cold, contorted on the sheets.

"Good God!!" cried Romanikha. She raced out and thundered down the stairs.

# PART II

# CHAPTER ONE

The city fell away from Borka in a smoky cloud and stretched out across the earth like some knifed stiff who had thrown his dead legs and head out beyond the now-distant horizon. The sky curved above Borka in a steep vault, a tangible firmament that was limpid and blue. Borka floated in the sky above the city. Huge and long, he glided in a blaze of hair whose shadow covered buildings. His body rang, strained in the wind. A strong wind lashed in the heights, rocked Borka. But it was not Borka above the city, it was Fear! Fear rose in the sky, covered buildings with its shadow, whirled in the wind. It fixed its disfigured eye on the city, dark beneath it and yellow with dust and sun in the distance, where its swift shadow had not yet reached. The flimsy roofs bent beneath that shadow. In an instant they would collapse on the crowded rooms, where people live like cockroaches. The little people huddled, trembled. Why they were all trembling they did not know—each had his own reason.

Fear swelled and shot higher. Far below, the city was dying, scratching at the sky with antennas and wires. It covered the weals and scars of its streets with soot and, from the first wall to the last, trembled with Fear.

To the right of the fire and smoke rose Woe. In a black column Woe arched out of the earth. The vault of the sky constricted Woe. No matter how sharply it bent, Woe could not find room.

To the left, Misfortune ascended like a wall, poured down on the buildings.

Fear raged, rumbled in the wind. To the right moved

Woe, to the left rose Misfortune.

The city sent the prods of scattered spires into the sky and stared down from these spires like stars, lidless like cockroach eyes, understanding nothing. And people trembled all through the city. Why they were all trembling the didn't know—each had his own reason.

\* \* \*

The first to notice the flying figures was the former watchman who had been kicked out of the morgue for drunkenness and—in his business—morbid sensitivity. This sensitivity of his reached the point that the watchman would sob and grieve over every bunch of corpses they brought him from each floor of the huge insane asylum. The watchman would sob, grieve, and then run down to the store for a bottle, to drink in memory of the deceased. Naturally, he was not much good for work. So they canned him, and the watchman was left without a job and without means of liquid sustenance.

He was in no hurry to find himself a new watchman's job—they needed watchmen everywhere. Just look how many thieves have sprung up and, thank God, there are more every year. You just cannot keep up. But just who you are guarding against, now that is a tricky question. These days everyone looks like a thief, thinks like a thief. The whole thing is, whose thief is he? If you do not know him, you have got to do your duty, grab him and drag him to court—that is only right. If he is one of yours, you can't do a thing, except maybe help him, assist to the best of your ability. And then, who is going to pay an honest man his salary anyway?

But the old man didn't want to steal yet. What was wrong with him? Whence this sensitivity, this cursed scrupulousness that has appeared in his soul and devours him? He guessed vaguely: was it not from when that stiff gave it to him with the radio? Clearly, it was from then precisely. Not only did the stiff mess up his head, he decorated him with a conscience too, the scoundrel. What kind of watchman has a conscience? He cannot work any more. In short, he is an invalid. That is what they made of him.

The old man contemplated his now conscience-crippled soul and looked at the sky, waiting for the store to open. Not a single cloud in the sky, and the sun burned brighter. It was really too much for the old man there on the steps, and he had twenty minutes more to wait.

"I'll keep the blasted thing in check another three days or so," he thought of his conscience, "and then that's enough, I'll go to work. It's time to steal."

They still were not about to open the store, though swollen, sleepy women with satchels and string bags still empty, flapping in the wind, had gathered by the doors.

"What is this?" the watchman thought slowly. "In a minute they'll open, and it'll be—here, take your kolbasa. And I've got a whole three hours to whistle away yet, until eleven. If only Fyodor doesn't carry anyone out of the outbuilding."

He rememberd the quiet and cool of the morgue, and it grieved, crushed the old man completely.

"Thanks a lot," he thought of the runaway corpses. "I hang around with you all that time and that's how you go and show your gratitude.... Swine!"

The old man looked at the sky again and suddenly dropped the hand-rolled cigarette from his weak, senile mouth. Above the city, in the sun's strong, oblique light, a body, terrible in its vastness, stretched from beyond the last buildings. The buildings bent their thin window panes and their old, crumbling plaster walls covered with large chalk scrawls. They seemed small, oppressed beneath the inordinate weight ready to collapse on them all. Black, swelling in smoky waves, as if half the city were burning in that direction, the body stretched. It turned its pale face with motionless, cataractous eyes and smoky jaws, an infernal maw yawning in the sky....

The cigarette smoked on the old man's worn-out pants, burning a brown spot, but the old man did not notice. From behind the store, which had been reroofed twice and still leaked, a second figure moved out, darker than the other one. It rose right into the blue firmament....

"Portents," whispered the old man. "Here it is, the day has come." And he saw the third figure pouring down on the city. "They'll crush all in their path...."

"You going crazy, Gramps, ha?" asked one woman. "You've burned through."

"His head got scorched in the sun. Look how he's staring at the sky," remarked a gloomy-looking citizen standing right by the door, quite unable to bring himself to take a single step toward the old man about to catch fire.

The woman was standing at the end of the line, so she had nothing to lose. Putting her enamel pail on the ground, she went up to him, bent over him, her stout face flooding crimson, and shook off the cigarette.

"Get up, or cover your head with something, you'll get scorched."

"There she is.... The day has come."

"The old man's cracked up," the citizen concluded, looking up just in case. Did he see something? Why no, nothing there, the sky was clear and hot.

Of the whole crowd that gathered thick by the store and pressed against its still-locked doors, only the old man saw the portents, saw them and was horrified. The old man looked around at the line and could not understand. No one was goggling at the sky, or clutching his head. No one threw his satchel down and ran off down the street, or rent his shirt and jacket, publicly confessing the sins that lay like millstones upon his heart. And the old man knew for a fact that those sins were there and lay upon their hearts. So what was the deal?

The old women were fuming as before, pushing each other away from the doors of the shop. The gloomy citizen tapped his fingernail on the crystal of his wristwatch, and even the eight-year-old boy who had pinched a ten-kopek piece from his mother for ice cream did not whimper with fright, but calmly and insolently looked the old man in the eye.

The old man figured it out. He got up, staggering on his numbed legs, and shuffled away from the crowd and the now quite superfluous store...

What was he thinking of? Was it about the fact that he had gone off his rocker like everyone in the hospital where he worked? But if there was anyone normal there, it was probably one of the patients—the doctors were all crazy. Or perhaps he was thinking of something else. But he was miserable, and he shuffled miserably down the street.

\* \* \*

Marusia was no longer to be found. She could not glance up into the deep sky above the city and could no longer be surprised when she descried the two old women flying like two black columns—the very women who had saved her twice from the Evil One. She could never be surprised again, much less scream—or sigh when Borka, her friend not long ago, who saw everything and suffered for everything, tore above the city like Fear. Marusia could not see that, much less scream—nor could she sigh beneath the heavy earth. The Evil One came a third time and destroyed her soul. There was no one to defend her the third time. She was supposed to defend herself, but she could not...

\* \* \*

That day no one spoke of the family that had so quickly vanished from this life. The room was empty, sealed by the police. And only one person in the building remembered Marusia, in fact only one person in the whole, huge city, which covered half the earth with asphalt and stone. Old lady Romanikha remembered, even had a little cry once in awhile. She was scared. Romanikha was scared not for herself, but for the dead Marusia, scared for the whole city, from whose memory people vanished so quickly.

Romanikha's own husband had died just recently. And though they had lived in harmony, and she probably even loved him, she did not grieve much then. Her husband was ill for a long time before his death, so long that he was a torment to everyone, and most of all to himself and her. During that long, horrible time, when he was suffering and her soul screamed itself sick, she stopped grieving for the first time and was even sort of glad that they had no children, that there was no one else to suffer, to watch how her husband tried to die but did not know how. There was no one else to suffer, just the neighbors in the next room cursing and waiting for his death, for when the groans would finally cease and the door stop slamming in the night. But then the neighbors were just two old women. It was time for them to die too...

But her husband was still ill. Night would come and he would get really bad. He would lie there all shrivelled up, and stretch his dry, dark hands across the blanket like old twigs. And on nights like that a smell would fill the room, as if they had left the door to a tomb ajar. Then suddenly he would be better. He'd get up, walk around the room and ask to be taken outside. But even then she was not glad. She no longer hoped. She knew it would not be long, soon he would be worse again.

One day like that, when death retreated, and the dying man revived, even sort of started to hope, as he always hoped, no matter how much he suffered later, Romanikha took her husband outside. They went slowly down the stairs, step by step, standing long on the landings, until they had gone down all the steps, all the way from the fourth floor. And outside the sick man wept when he saw the sky and the day. He went up to a lilac bush, which grew behind the fence, beneath the yardman's window. He stretched out his hand, so thin it would have easily gone between the fence boards, and pinched off a leaf. He looked at that leaf, pressed it to his dead lips.

He walked farther and looked at everything—at the building, and at the windows in the building. He peered at people, and when he spied some stone beneath his feet he trembled. He had not walked very far at all, but he was already tired. Romanikha felt his palm grow sweaty. It grew softer, and wet.

They turned back, entered the lane that led into the courtyard from the street, and started to turn the corner of the building, when her husband suddenly stopped. He was looking at the door of the service entrance. Romanikha looked too. She was surprised. The door, which was always locked and even blocked with boards, was now ajar, collapsed against the wall, leaving a wide black crevice. Why, who would have opened it? Romanikha had lived there for forty years, and as long as she had been there, the door had always been locked, no one ever used that entrance.

"Come on, what's there to see?" she asked. She was frightened because her husband looked at that door so. He was about to move on and stopped again, quietly, as if to himself, and said, "That's my place..."

\* \* \*

He didn't go outside again—he got worse and worse. The doors slammed in the night, and the ambulance came. But what was it ambulating for? He was dead. The orderlies took him and buried him themselves, at public expense. He was sick so long and died so imperceptibly. Only the neighbors knew of it, and they did not mind at all...

Romanikha was left alone with her troubles. After her husband's death she started to regret not having children again—one misfortune disappears, others remain. She started buying candies with the last of her money. She always carried a worn paper bag now and treated the children on the street. But they would not take any. The children were afraid of her, afraid of this old woman with the terrifying face, so dark, like a Negro's. And if some did take a candy fearfully, they would throw it away around the corner or smash the glaze with a brick and look at the powder that was left, with which the old woman tried to poison them.

In the whole building, only Marusia spoke to her. She was affable and helped Romanikha where she could, as no one had ever helped her—neither children nor grown-ups.

On the day the portents appeared above the city, Romanikha went to visit a distant relative. Once she got there, she was tired and spent the whole day sitting at the table drinking tea and eating cheap caramels, worse than the ones she carried in her paper bag. She complained of life and listened to complaints herself. It turns out that everyone lives badly: when you have a husband and when you do not, when you have no children and when your children are growing up— they are all brats now anyway, and when they are grown they finally get what they have been asking for and land in prison. "What is this?" Romanikha could make no sense of it. "There should be someone in the city who's living well. Otherwise why put the city up?" It turns out that even the generals are not living well now. Her relative told how one actually shot himself in his five-room apartment. And another man, some big cheese, practically the head of the lot, was such a heavy drinker that they sewed up his pipes so he would not drink any more. Bet he is not the only one.

"Why is that?" Romankha thought, and could not understand it. All the old people are on pensions now, or sitting in the poorhouse. It is a rare bird who feeds himself, and you think it is easy for him? No, it is not easy. The pension is small. There it is—you get twenty rubles.[1] Just try to live on that. And the young people? All hooligans. And if they are not hooligans, then they are just plain fools—they go off to the building sites of communism[2] with the criminals. And so many of them —the young people—are sitting in insane asylums.

The old women continued their dreary conversation for a long time, until it grew dark outside the window. Romanikha put down her cup and hurried home. It is not easy for an old person to make it home at night.

Though she hurried, tried to walk faster, she approached her house in pitch darkness. She walked down the empty, windswept lane and had almost made it to her entryway when she looked up and froze. In the dark wall before her, a window shone. Her window.

No one could be there. There was no one who would be there. She froze and, without knowing what she was doing—instead of running to the police station or knocking at her neighbors' door—she went up the stairs to her apartment, to her room, her heart affright. It was empty and black in the apartment. Just the door to her room was open. A lamp was burning, and her deceased husband was looking for something in the room.

He turned around, saw his wife, her white face covered with lengthened wrinkles showing white, and came towards her... Then something seemed to cover her, to pass darkly before her, and the light appeared again. Only now the deceased was behind her, walking down the corridor, out of the apartment, like a dense shadow.

"Wait!" She tried to keep up with him in the dark.

He walked away, he did not turn around. She could hear him pounding down the steps.

"Wait!" Stumbling, bumping into walls, she went. She made it out to the stairway and started going down also. A door opened and slammed below.

Faster and faster she hurried down the stairs. She shoved the door open, sprang into the courtyard. Her husband was walking off around the corner, without turning back...

She ran over and saw the yardman in his lighted lodge, whistling something, tying up a besom.

"Hey, Romanikha, I just saw your old man," he said calmly and happily. "Did he get better? He went that way." He pointed his finger with its thick yellow nail. "He really walks fast, guess he's pretty healthy."

Silent, she rushed into the lane. Empty. Beyond it, the street, lit dimly by a lamp, was also empty. She turned back to the building. The door to the service entrance stood wide open, still swinging, creaking.

## CHAPTER TWO

After the portents had appeared, after the sky above the city had been engulfed in flames, a dark time began. It had been red, but it became black, blacker than black smoke. Corpses marched upon the city. Decayed, putrid with corruption, the endless crowds marched. They marched on the city from the cemeteries and churchyards. The drowned walked out of the rivers, the knifed came from the woods, from those dreadful places they had lain many long years. A rumbling rose across the land.

And in the city itself the crosses fell in the cemeteries, the graves opened. They rose as all will rise who clamor for Judgement. The earth is filled with victims, with those who moan and cry out. They were risen...

The police, the whole Committee[1] —all the gallant young men—blanched simultaneously and rushed about in terror with their pistols and iron handcuffs. What was to be done? There were thousands of police, and there were tanks, machine guns, but the earth was packed with the murdered. They had murdered them themselves—they knew there were a lot.

In the parks the trees suddenly started rocking, the leaves falling—there were corpses there too. These were not parks, they were cemeteries. Many of the city's cemeteries had disappeared in the red time. They destroyed them, leveled the earth. And they sowed grass, so the cemeteries looked like parks. They smashed the gravestones, burned the crosses. It looked green and sophisticated, as if we had no dead, no mass graves from plague and cholera. It turned out there was a lot that we did not have. Asphalt roads crawled through cemeteries, over human bones, and parks rustled—over bones.

The asphalt swelled and split—the corpses stood. Scattered bones were overgrown with dead flesh. Now they were everywhere—on all the streets and squares, in all the gardens and parks, in all the houses, in the whole city. What was to be done?

The inhabitants ran from their homes and apartments, right in front of the tank treads whose heavy metal thundered through all the streets. They screamed beneath them as they were torn to bits by prehensile pinions, and blood ran in the roads in dirty, black streams.

They ran back, climbed up to the roofs through attics and up fire escapes. Soon the whole city was on the roofs. The buildings drifted toward the horizon, and the roofs all moved. The people were saved from mortal ruin.

Romanikha sat in a crowd of tenants on the steep pitch of the old, galvanized iron roof with its dull, peeling paint, holding on to an antenna rough with dust and rust. There was no more than a meter to the narrow eaves trough which hung above the lane. Beyond it, at the bottom of the rumbling gap between the buildings, Romanikha saw fantastic things.

A corpse sprang out of a wall, black, hacked almost in two. Frightfully, he bared his big teeth, looked around and rushed down the lane bent double, helping himself along with his long arms, which reached nearly to the ground. Even up above she could hear his dead claws scrabbling on the pavement.

Romanikha shuddered in horror and, freeing one hand, quickly crossed herself. God be with us!

Below, a car raced past, screeching rubber on the

turn. Its windows were broken and the crumpled radiator spewed something dark. At the end of the narrow lane it grazed the corner, knocking a brick out of the wall. Dropping its left headlight with a clank, it disappeared.

A man in a blue police jacket ran past, his boots pounding sharply, his torn collar bouncing like a rag on his back, smeared with dirt. His numbed face continually turned back from where he had run, and his hand groped at his black throat. He had scarcely disappeared around the corner when such a howl arose that up above they all shuddered, and Romanikha almost let the pole of the antenna out of her hands. God be with us!

Only now did Romanikha understand from whence the frozen waves came that entered her, that stained the sky in her eyes, that clutched at her old heart, that broke in her breast. Above the city, in the smoky half-light of the fire, hung the cry of thousands of mouths torn open in horror.

Now, stretching their necks, many of the tenants looked down. The children crept to the very edge, squealed, fought for places. Mothers cursed and crawled down the steep slopes after their children. But the children ran away and started fighting again. One child fell, tumbled, and with a choked cry, flew down, down the dark, slanting, stone wall. He had not struck the asphalt yet, and his little body was whole. He was still alive when his mother's howl split the street. She threw herself after him, but they did not let her go. She broke free, creeping closer and closer to the edge, and the hands which tore her dress could not hold her. She was on the very edge when the tenants who had raced to her aid managed to grab her firmly, and she froze on the warm, worn roof, and grew quiet.

Romanikha saw this, but understood very little. And woe did not touch her at all. When all perish, why grieve? She sat there; she did not even rush to help, though at one time she had been kind.

Someone's scream echoed once again down below. A man walked slowly, flattening himself against the wall, with a broken arm and a bloody rag in place of an eye. It was impossible to make out either the uniform he wore or his maimed face, only the red rag and the black, gaping mouth. The man screamed continuously, and the scream entered him like a stake, and wrenched the teeth from his gums. The man shielded himself with his good arm, not noticing the pistol clutched in his hand.

Suddenly the walls trembled, and the whole sky around the people crowding the roofs shook. A black shadow appeared. The corpses marched. The dark faces were paralyzed in corruption. Their decaying and decayed feet marched with a heavy step, and the whole city trembled. The leaders only looked with frozen faces at the maimed man, pressed in pain and terror to the wall, and walked past in a dreadful crowd. And new ones passed. Suddenly a howl went up among the dead bodies. A corpse, completely naked, his hair flopping dead around his head, rushed out of the crowd.

"He's the one who murdered me!"

Several other lifeless faces dashed after him.

"And me... And me..."

The first was already next to the man, who still shielded himself with his arm. The corpse seized it and in one jerk tore it from the shoulder, together with the pistol clutched in its hand. Romanikha heard the snap of broken tendons. The man collapsed on the stones, and several corpses rent him limb from limb.

"He murdered me!" They rent him.

Romanikha closed her eyes. She was not terrified, but she felt so ill that she thought she would lose consciousness. God be with us!

Just then something started crashing on the roof next door, across the lane. Romanikha had scarcely opened her eyes when she saw a tenant of that building, his head shaking and beating on the rumbling iron, roll faster and faster towards the edge. No one was near him, and no one managed to hold him back once he had lost consciousness. Striking the gutter he froze and flew down with it. His heavy body struck the stones.

Then suddenly Romanikha heard a low song. Someone next to her was singing. Turning, she saw a merry old man. In a quiet senile wheeze he sang:

> Bravely march we off to war
> For the Soviet regime...

The old man sat hugging a short iron flue that stuck up out of the roof. Apparently he was not grieved at all.

"We'll all end up down there," he said, sizing up the route the fallen man had taken. He started singing something again, spitting in the pauses between couplets on the police running past down below. Sometimes the wind carried his spittle down on the corpses, but it made no difference to either group. Only the old man was distressed each time he heard he got a corpse.

"Hit one of our guys again."

Romanikha had not seen him earlier. Apparently the old man had climbed up there not long before.

"Well, ma'am," the old man said, noticing that

Romanikha was looking at him, "here's a nice day for you, I guess."

She did not answer, but this did not distress the old man in the least, and he continued, "Nice day. I've been waiting for it a long time, and now it's here."

He said this with pleasure and, not forgetting to hold onto the flue, even stretched out on the iron roof as if he were getting a tan.

"Before I dropped in here, know where I was?" He looked at Romanikha with wise eyes, not at all crazy. "Bet you can't guess... at the Metropolitan's."

Romanikha almost lost her head from the old man's cheerfulness and brazen lies, and did not notice how the fear in her ebbed.

"Oh, you're lying," she said.

Not only did the old man not take offense at these words, he broke into his merriest smile, as if he had been complimented for heaven knows what.

"No, I'm not lying, ma'am, there's no point in my lying. Especially since for lies, as for other sins, one may have to answer, ve-ery, very soon." The old man motioned around them with his free hand. "This is a real doomsday... And I really was at the Metropolitan's. I was going to climb up on his roof, like I did here. Enormous house, and then, so I thought, a holy place, strong enough to withstand the Evil Spirit. Well, I was just going to go in. I pushed the door open, thinking, I've got to get up to the attic somehow, when I see, all the way up the stairs, a whole crowd of people. Most of them in uniform. And in the back, someone in black. At first I decided that they were arresting the Metropolitan. Then I looked—he's walking around and the guys in uniform are all generals. What goings-on... There was no sense even thinking about climbing up. I ran down the street, and the corpses were coming towards me. Really spooky ones too... And I've seen corpses myself. Nearly all my life I've been watchman at the morgue. I've gone through a lot for them." Here the old man felt his head and sighed. "But that's okay, we get intelligent folks in our morgue, you might say, not like these..." The watchman got a more comfortable grip with his numbed hand and continued, no longer addressing just Romanikha, but the other tenants who had gathered around. "So when this unwashed crowd descended—this is it, I think, now they'll put me out of the way, and I won't have to steal or look for work. I got canned a little while ago. My knees had just started to fold up under me, and I thought I'd hit the dirt so it wouldn't be so easy to deal with me, when I notice that no one's touching me. Apparently no one wants me... Well, I get out of the way, thinking, what do I need to do most of all? It was awful how many of them were barging along, and all going where I'd slipped out of. I looked around— Holy Mother! The generals had pushed the Metropolitan out in front of them, and he was shaking so bad all over that his cross bounced on his chest. He held his hand out in front of him with another cross, and stumbled through a prayer. He made the sign of the cross, made the cross over the corpses, but in vain..."

"Why didn't they shoot?" someone behind Romanikha asked in surprise.

"Ha... shoot those things?" The old man laughed, pleased. "Just try it. They could shoot till they didn't know their own mother. What's a bullet to a dead man? Not a good spit, that's what. He's already gotten his. Run him over with a tank—you won't crush him. Maybe if you smear him with a cannon..." The old man fell to thinking, looking at the low, wind-whipped sky. "I couldn't say, haven't seen it. Yeah, so he made the sign of the cross over them. But they aren't afraid of anything, not even a cross."

"Obviously, the cross was in the wrong hands—the ecclesiast had no sanctity," said Romanikha quickly, surprising herself. She'd never been a believer.

"Right," the old man agreed, "that's what had happened."

Then something rumbled just below the roof, and pale faces appeared in the narrow dormers. New tenants climbed out of the attic.

"Damn," the old man sighed with relief. "I thought they'd got here already... So he made the sign of the cross over them, but what's that to them? And one of the departed yells, 'You're the devil and your cross is demonic!' And he was right—the cross burst into flames, blazed with fire, like a demonic star. Then the corpses rushed them. The generals were quickly subdued, they broke their necks, but the Metropolitan—no way.

"At first I thought the Almighty would help him, and then I see it's the other way around. They tore off the cassock he was wearing and underneath was a red shirt. Right—it turned out to be the Evil One. So I'd almost climbed up on the roof with the Devil. That wouldn't have been so bad, I'd have held out. But the Evil One was fighting with them, sent one then another reeling. Then they overcame him, fell on him in a heap. He thrashed around on the ground and vanished..."

"Go on, you're lying," a sullen eight-year-old boy declared from behind his mother's back. The old man's mouth dropped at such a turn. He looked at the boy and immediately recognized him—the boy who had pinched the ten-kopek piece from his mother for ice cream. Calmly and insolently he looked the old man in the eye.

"Holy Mother, protect us from that!" the old man said sadly, slapping his thigh. They all smiled, and someone even laughed.

"I guess the Metropolitan must have been a big thief, for the Evil One to have turned into him," said Romanikha.

"Oh, they're all thieves there... sitting pretty." The eight-year-old's mother shook her fist angrily. "They should work in our shoes for a while."

"That wouldn't do any good," a man said, offended—an elderly, intelligent-looking man with a straw hat on, and a shiner under one eye. "There are some truly saintly men among the clergy, I once knew..."

"It's all lies—there are no saints, it's all fabrication," said a gloomy citizen with conviction. The watchman remembered him too—the same man who had been standing first in line at the store.

"Perhaps there are no corpses down below either?" the old man grinned. "What are you sitting up here for?"

The citizen was about to answer, but only moved his lips and turned away even more gloomily.

"That's right," the old man exulted, "better keep quiet."

\* \* \*

It was quiet beneath the gray, ash-covered walls of the municipal crematorium, whose frightening stench spread far and wide. There were no people there. In the huge, dying city, where the howl and moan of mortal perdition had split the very earth, the crematorium stood empty and deserted. The frightened workers had scattered that morning, and now the wind carried scraps of paper and brittle, twisted leaves through the open gates. The dark slabs of the columbarium[2] stuck up in the sand in crooked rows, huddling close behind the high walls. Faces, and more faces, of the dead buried here, in these walls.

The coarse-grained sand scrunched. A man was walking, stealing along the walls with their innumerable faces. He was pale, frightened to death. He wore a rumpled civilian jacket and blue uniform trousers with a red stripe running down them, also rumpled and torn at the knee. He stopped and listened. Outside, beyond the wall, the dying city roared like a tortured body. He listened again—it was quiet all around. Except outside, the expiring city moaned. The city, occupied by the dead— a city of death.

The man remembered, so long ago, in those far distant years they do not like to write about in books now —we made mistakes, they say (though as a whole, the policies were correct)—in those far distant, youthful years, he had worked as an operative himself and carried out all of those policies. Today's Committee was called something else then. But then, all sorts of names were changed so many times you could not keep track of them, even though everything remained as it had been. Only there used to be more work. And how they worked, not at all like now! They worked with zest, with spirit. Now if you do hit some prisoner, you do it without any style or satisfaction. So, you slash his puss with a live wire. It's just not the same. But before... Ah, before! Before, they would stack those prisoners right up to the ceiling in the basement of headquarters after interrogation. It went on like that every day, with no holidays. Now that's work! You weren't ashamed to be called an operative.

He remembered how he had driven through these gates in a truck, opened the doors into the hall of the crematorium with one blow. He remembered the faces of the relatives of the dead, and the faces of the attendants. And especially the sweet face of the young directress in her red kerchief. The Youth Brigade had sent her here.[3] She was pretty. Ah, if only there had been more time... But as it was, you grab them by the breasts, squeeze them, grope around a bit under their skirts and boot them in the ass—move it! True, he still found time. He was no snivelling activist.[4] But that was later, when he had been transferred to another job... They would just cuss at the crowd and drive them off. And then some other guys from headquarters would drive in with another truck, hang a lock on the gate, mount a guard, and the work would start—to burn all those that had been heaped in stacks at headquarters. The smoke belched out for weeks. How many he'd personally burned himself! But they were not alive—they were dead!

The man remembered and stole along the walls with their innumerable faces. The ones in the walls at least had an inscription of some sort, a photograph, but where are the inscriptions for those he had burned? The man smiled to himself. What inscription? There are their ashes, buried in that far corner, lots of them. They poured it in sacks, carried it in sacks. They had to dig a pit three meters deep. And they didn't always have time to play around, so they would just leave them, all those they had burned. The attendants would clean up the ashes later. What they had done with them he still did not know. And why should he know? So he could set up a monument to his work or what? Though it would not be a bad idea if they had put up something somewhere.

If Borka had walked through those gates just then and seen the man in the rumpled civilian jacket and the blue uniform trousers with the red stripe running down them, beneath that jacket he would have immediately recognized the investigator, the very one who had interrogated Borka and made him confess to murder. In these few days the investigator had aged considerably, and he was not young to start with. He was decked out in that jacket for some reason—but you cannot escape from what has happened. In any case, Borka was not there. Like Fear he soared above the city. Fear was there.

The investigator stopped, and his eyes swam in darkness. In that corner, *that* corner—the earth rose. What is this? They aren't rising from the ashes, are they?

A piece of turf was dislodged from the trampled ground with its yellowed grass. It shot up a half-meter and fell to one side, scattering dry earth. And in that spot, black smoke went up, rose higher than the walls, higher than the black chimney of the crematorium. A gray lump fell from the heights of the cloud—and the first corpse arose. The investigator fixed his mad gaze upon him and immediately recognized him—his first arrest. It was not he who had interrogated him. He was still a sub then. Others did the interrogating, and he did whatever they ordered. He remembered him—his first arrest—lying in blood on the floor. They had interrogated him hard, but he did not confess. He was a stubborn one. He remembered that they gave him a rifle cleaning-rod, that he heated it in the fire. It got crimson, then yellow-red. He thrust it up the anus of the naked man, who still lay on the floor in a pool of blood. And to this day he remembered, he will never forget, how the man yelled, writhed, tearing his intestines on the cleaning rod... That is how his first arrest died.

Overhead, massing damply from the ash, another corpse fell and moved slowly towards the investigator. He was familiar too. He had immediately confessed, repented of all the things he had not done. But then they felt like a little fun. They poured gunpowder in his ear and nose and lit it. And now the dead man was missing half his face, and the bones were exposed. And there's another one, and another... All stealing up to him.

The investigator was stepping back, retreating before all his victims, when another dead man sprang out from beneath his feet. The attendants had apparently buried his dust there. The corpse scraped his teeth together and seized hold of the investigator's leg. As if in his sleep, the investigator tore himself away—as if he could have gotten away. He tried to free himself, looked at the corpse with a numbed gaze, but did not remember him at all—it is not true what they say about an executioner remembering all of his victims. He did not remember anything. And he is no executioner, he simply did his duty. There is such a thing as duty.

The dead man tore the strong trouser leg to shreds and then sliced a piece of meat from the shin. The wound burned. The investigator's body jerked, he screamed in agony—as if someone would really help. And in that far corner where the ashes were buried, new corpses stood. They rose up from the road and beneath the trees. They all, all, raced towards the murderer.

The investigator's heart bounded. The blood thumped in his back, rushed in his throat. He beat them off, but hundreds of canines sank into his flesh, and hundreds of hands rent him. One, a little one with once-red hair turned green in the earth, traced a secant on the investigator's belly with his tooth. The investigator felt how light it was in his stomach, how hot, and his legs flooded with the heat. He tried again to beat them off, but his hands grew empty and light. The earth bounded into his face. The investigator had fallen.

* * *

The whole long day it thundered in the streets of the city. Romanikha sat on the very edge of the roof. The watchman sat there too, and no longer told any stories. People were still coming, new tenants still sought rescue on the roofs. But there was no more room there, and the beams beneath the old iron creaked. In a moment they would collapse. Shots still slammed through the city, but in the uneasy wind that rushed across the roofs, then rose straight up, they no longer heard the clank and thunder of the tanks. The tanks were silent, and through the whole city the dead marched and marched.

Not a single bird traced circles in the smoky-purple sky. It was so empty and frightful there that the watchman tried not to look at it. He sat with his legs tucked under him, mumbling something to himself. And the beams beneath the old iron roof trembled. In a moment the roof would collapse.

Several policemen ran past down the lane, their hobnailed boots clattering loudly. One of them, already at the very edge of the lane, looked up and saw the crowd of people on the roofs. He was not surprised. No, he had stopped being surprised long ago. He just stopped. "Right," he thought to himself, and tore off his cap and rushed to the entrance. In a minute he appeared, strong and sweaty, with gnashing teeth, in the dormer window. There was no place to climb further—people were sitting everywhere. Closest to him was a fat woman in a blue knitted jacket and torn stockings. The woman's worn-out shoes stood on the dormer slat, and the policeman, grabbing the strap on one, threw them down into the attic's darkness, streaked with dust-colored rays.

"Just where are you climbing to? Where? Can't you see, there are people sitting here!" The angry woman bickered, but she did not yell too loud, scared by the policeman's hunted look. He paid no attention to what she said. He was not up to that. He tore his pistol from its brown holster, shiny with wear, and jabbing it in her wide back, ordered, "Now move it, you shit."

The woman gasped and shoved herself out of the way in horror, forcing the tenants sitting nearby to slide back.

"Hey, who's pushing over there?" people yelled over their shoulders. "Don't push, you scum, or we'll fall."

The policeman stepped over the woman, caught his boot in someone's bundle, swore, grabbed the bundle with one hand and, scattering blue and pink rags, threw it over the heads into the lane.

"Artishchev!" reached them from below. "Ar-ti-shchev!"

Artishchev froze and waited until the boots clattered down below again, and it grew quiet.

"Now move it," he said again, kicking someone with his boot. The people were sitting so closely that they could not make room and, frightened, only moved to one side, shoving their neighbors, not settling down for long, only until the backs of those behind them shoved them back again. Beneath the roof and somewhere deep within the house the rafters creaked long and loud.

Artishchev stopped above Romanikha, screening the sun caught in his hair. There was nowhere further to walk. He stuck the barrel of the pistol, which smelled of burning, in her face.

"Get up."

"Why?" Romanikha was surprised; she saw only a black shadow over her, and did not even make out what she was being threatened with.

"You'll find out. Now, pronto."

"Leave me alone," she said, still not understanding a thing. "Quit pestering."

"Why you..." And with the heavy burnished steel, he hit her in the face. Romanikha screamed, stopped short and covered her face with her hands. Blood dripped fast between her fingers.

"What are you doing, you hoodlum!" yelled Romanikha's neighbor, looking at the policeman with fear and hatred.

"Good people, look! That man's driving this woman away! He wants to sneak into her spot!" yelled someone else.

"Shut up!" Artishchev turned and fired over their heads. It fell quiet instantly. The people were silent, though they looked at him with hatred. And no one intervened. Who wants to die?

"Get up," he repeated, and raised his pistol. Somewhere behind their backs, a child choked and cried. He was the only one who cried. The people were silent, hushed. Who wants to die?

The shot, which echoed in the street and down the lane, distracted the watchman from his thoughts. He turned, looked—and instantly understood everything. Now, right now, that policeman, sweaty and dark, will fire a shot in his neighbor's face. Right now... Right through her palms and fingers. The watchman threw himself at him, tearing the skirts of his tarpaulin jacket out from under the people next to him. He tackled him as hard as he could around his boots, dirty and dusty, all smeared with blood.

Romanikha heard a cry. She took her hands from her face, smashed by the steel. The sun reeled behind a large, black head. The policeman toppled over the eaves trough into the void, down the dark, stone walls, slanting over the blood-blackened asphalt.

"Let's get away from here," said the watchman, panting.

Romanikha herself found the roof disgusting by now, and the corpses did not scare her.

"How can we get through?"

Around them, everyone continued to sit silently. Even the child wasn't crying any more. He had settled down. One citizen in a gray jacket and a shirt and tie, sitting on the far side from Romanikha, heaved a loud sigh of relief and, taking out a clear plastic comb, blew on the teeth and combed his hair. "Dmitry," Romankha read the tattoo on his hand.

"This way," the watchman called, and began stealing along the very edge toward the fire escape.

As soon as they got down, something cracked loudly up above, and a crash shook the house so that the windows splintered in all the neighboring buildings. The roof collapsed. Dust, like smoke from a fire, rose in a thick shadow over the building's fissured walls.

## CHAPTER THREE

Again three suns rose over the city. It should have been evening. And night should have come. But it did not. Three suns flashed summer lightning, smoky and red. The holiday was over the city again. Again woe began.

The watchman looked round at the three slate shadows that ran after him, springing over the stones. He spat, "There are those damned things again, their strength is coming back. Look how they've flared up." Shading his eyes with his palm, he looked into the sky, as at portraits of government leaders.

The time had passed when portraits hung on every building in the whole city. There were many portraits, thousands—but they were not in sight, as if there were no authority in the city, and no regime at all. And the portraits were all different—drawn any old way. Disorder. Flags do not help, no matter how many there are. They gave it a lot of thought, and finally came up with something. Now three suns rise on big holidays, and there is a portrait on each one.[1] The holiday looked fervidly through the three suns above the city and drove away the clouds, melted the snow if necessary. It makes July out of May, and from November, a quiet, dry September. It is comfortable, and on a day like that it is nice to go to the demonstrations.[2] But those shadows! Well, what are shadows anyway. Only the cats were afraid of them and scrambled up the trees in terror. They howled there, and tore their wide sides on the branches.

The watchman and Romanikha walked through the city, and no one touched them. The crowds of corpses walked past. True, the watchman was a little afraid of meeting his own, from the morgue. But then he figured, if they had borne him any grudges, they would have paid them off when they cracked him on the noggin. The old man felt his head—just about nothing, it had stopped hurting.

Romanikha walked slower and slower. She peered at the horrible crowds passing by to see if she could spot her husband. But no matter how long she looked, he was not there. Only strangers passed by. And who could bring themselves to turn to the dead and ask? So she stood on the edge of the road and looked, looked, peered at the faces...

"You going to be long?" The watchman was angry. "We have to find a hacksaw and you're staring off somewhere. Are they going to give you a saw, or what?"

"Why do you need the saw?" Romanikha asked, but still looked, looked...

"Why?! Because we have to saw off that piece of shit!" The old man pointed to the spire of the biggest, the most enormous building in the city, whose glass star glittered in the sky.

"Ah..."

" 'Ah, ah...,' you just don't listen." The watchman was still angry, but all he thought about was how they could get to that star. He had been thinking about it quite a while ago, when he was still sitting on the roof. He knew that it would be difficult to do. But it had to be done, or else the Evil One with his demonic star would conquer.

The watchman did not tell her everything. When he had walked away down the street, hugging the wall, a dead woman from the crowd had stopped him. The old man had lost his nerve at first, and taken fright:

her mouth—an open wound—was clotted with blood. One cheek was bitten through, and the edges sewn together later, apparently. "While the Evil One lives," she said, "we shall not conquer. While the fire of his star chars the sky, no one will be saved, as we were not..." She said that, and a heavy tear rolled out from beneath her dead eyelid...

Now the watchman walked, and looked for a hacksaw. He glanced around at Romanikha, but Romanikha was waiting for her husband, who any moment might appear from among the bodies. She decided that she would go with him, die right there, and dead, go with him, her dead husband. She would commit suicide and not leave him now. Only, her husband was not there. Suddenly Romanikha understood. She should look where he had disappeared that time, in the black, rumbling crevice. The dead man had managed to come to her, and she, still alive, would go to him happily.

"I'm going back."

The old man was about to express surprise, but he looked at Romanikha and did not ask any questions. She has her own troubles, her own burdens, and he would have to get along without help, apparently.

"Goodbye."

"Good luck." He went on alone beneath the three evil suns.

More and more often he came across living people, those who had killed no one, and who had nothing to fear from the dead. Only when an armored tank thundered past or a policeman leaped out with a pistol did they hide. They were afraid of them—their own fanatics were worse than wild beasts.

In the center of the city it was quiet—no tanks, no risen corpses. Only the glass in the windows was broken out, and mutilated bodies clung to the hot stones. Mostly military, but some civilians too, in identical dark jackets, now dirty and torn. They were clearing them off the road, and strewing the streams of blood with sand.

There, in the center, the old man met Fomka, with his head bandaged and his arm in a sling. Fomka's head was bandaged with a piece of crisp, starched tablecloth with yellow, washed-out spots. Fomka, stupefied, did not recognize the old man and would have walked right past if the old man had not grabbed him by the shoulder.

"Oy!" yelled Fomka, wincing all over in pain. He closed one eye filled with tears and only then could he recognize the old man.

It turned out that the terrified Fomka had skipped out to the writers' house and stupidly climbed up on the roof to escape like everyone else. By that time the roof was just packed with writers, many of them well-known and even famous, so it was not surprising that Fomka, like many others, was not greeted too politely. They attempted to drive him away, throw him off the roof. Someone suggested over and over that they check to see if Fomka had a membership card. Fomka threw that one off the roof himself—but maybe it was not him, because a disorderly scuffle started up, and there was no time to make it out. Suddenly all the writers started fighting at once, among themselves and together against Fomka and the others. At that very moment the roof crashed down, collapsing into the marvelous writers' library, and then, with books and shelves, on into the Oak Room of the writers' restaurant. They came down not only in the restaurant, but into the City Writers' Organization and the writers' club. Fomka himself landed in the restaurant. By sheer luck he survived, having come down on the gray head of an imposing writer whom he had seen many times on television, and whose programs he liked very much. But he could not remember his name just then.

"Where are you going?" the old man asked.

"How should I know?" sighed Fomka beneath the tight, starched band. "Home, probably, if the house is still standing."

"Hardly," said the old man doubtfully. "I don't think you'll find a single building in the city still standing, but then..."

Cannons hammered loudly outside the city, and yellow leaves falling from the trees, curled and dry, tapped on the pavement. The old man was in a hurry, and though he wanted to find a helper very much, and though it would probably be easier with help, he saw that Fomka would not be any good, he was not the right man.

"Well, I'm off," he said, and hurried down the street.

"You're off," Fomka answered, barely audibly.

The old man stopped by the ruined writers' house, behind whose walls the groans of wounded writers could still be heard. Here is where he would find a saw. Where else if not here? He climed over a solidly-constructed piece of cement wall lying in front of the entrance in the dust of broken plasterwork, and, swinging the heavy, tall door open with difficulty, went in. Inside it was just as light as on the street, only more debris of boards and brick. His steps rumbled across the twisted sheet metal, and the watchman looked around. In front of him, over to the now-exposed piece of wall, faced with dark oak panelling, which by some miracle retained its stained-glass windows, it was all blocked with the collapsed ceiling. To the left, in the corner, in the piles of debris, stood a tall-case clock with brass face and weights. To the right, an unhinged door showed dark. Groans could be heard behind the farther wall, and the voices of people working there and the clatter of breaking debris reached him.

"The cellar," the watchman decided and headed for the unhinged door. Turning left beyond the door and going downstairs past the undamaged elevator, the watchman ended up in the buffet,[3] rather than in the cellar. In the corner, a part of the ceiling collapsed on him, and through the breach trickled a light reflection of the three holiday suns. Going past the bar, which shone dimly with mirrors and bottles of French cognac, the old man found himself in the complete darkness of the corridor. An iron door at its very end was wide open, and the smell of paint and stifling, congealed darkness carried up from the cellar. The watchman found some matches in the pocket of his tarp, and tracing timid red flames, went in. He was not mistaken. Almost immediately, among the heaps of paper and all sorts of rubbish, which usually occupy the shelves of any storeroom, including literary ones, he found a whole box of tools. "Soon now," he thought. The match shone as two flames in his eyes. Up above, the volleys of artillery fire shuddered louder and louder.

\* \* \*

The enormous building rose before him, gray, of once-white stone, with arches, a spire, and a glass star. Lifted into the sky, its weight oppressed the thin glass of the neon "Grocery" sign which wound in ribbons on the red granite below. It was quiet. The old man went around the square and walked up to a side stairway. From the side, the whole building spilled out before the old man, raising, flaunting its dark statues high above him. They looked far beyond the city, where the rumbling thundered louder and louder. A half-naked man, wearing only stone pants, his whole body terribly strained, turned in that direction and waited for something. Stone children waited too, and collosal mothers, like frozen idols. Beyond their raised hands, gray walls pierced through with windows mounted up and fell away from the old man. Higher yet soared arches and balustrades with steep, thin spires, and above it all the beam of that glass star whirled away from him.

Climbing the stairway of the red granite plinth with its hash of broken railings, the watchman entered the building. Right there, on the tiles of the dark landing, two bodies lay stretched out, both in uniforms without shoulder straps, both with blackened faces and blue-veined tongues hanging out. Nearby lay a slain corpse in a torn, half-decayed shirt.

That surprised the old man, and he moved warily up the dark and booming stairway. The whole enormous building was full of sounds, rustling and whistling through its passages. Now somewhere down below, on the lower floors, which the old man had managed to get past, a piercing howl rushed madly about. It ceased abruptly, and its echo cried out through all the floors. Then, above him, almost immediately, something huge broke deafeningly into thousands of pieces, all ringing and scattering on the floor. Someone's feet crunched loudly and heavily down the whole stairway. On one of the upper floors, with a bridge to another wing, the old man saw someone running toward him. He thrust his hand in the toolbox and grabbed a hammer in his palm, sweaty with terror, but the man stopped when he saw the watchman and rushed into a side passage.

The old man climbed higher and higher. Through the thick walls, the rooms, floors, and passages he saw how high he hung above the city, above its ruined buildings, its ragged roofs, and above the flame of a new battle, whose din came closer and closer. The old man knew—it was the Evil One approaching.

The stairway ended. It stopped short in a corridor as dark as it was wide, a whole street, at the end of which shone a small window. The window was broken, and a damp and hazy draught came all the way down the corridor. The old man even shivered from its piercing strength, and drew the tarp closer around him. A new stairway. It was lighted from above with a heavy light from windows the old man could not see. Again, trembling intermittently, in little jolts, the steps ran downwards, disappeared behind the old man's tarp-covered back. Many steps, so many you could not count them all. A landing sank down and, rolling slightly, swung in front of him. Everything was empty. No one was there either, though sounds reached him from the shadows of the occupied building. The terrible sounds of a death house.

Again someone small and far away, crushed by the hard knot of dead stairways and passages, screamed and screamed.

The watchman was not afraid that the door to the attic would be locked—a whole box of tools would help him break the lock or saw it out of the door. But he did not have to do that: the attic door, covered with sheet iron, was open, and through the wide crack an attic dampness blew out onto the stairs.

"Night soon," thought the old man. Why he thought that all of a sudden he did not know himself—the three suns still shone through the window of the stairwell.

In the attic, as soon as he went in, something fell back from the door and disappeared into the depths, crunching over the thick layer of dross. The old man was bathed in a cold sweat and, pulling the hammer from the box, held it now at the ready. By two dusty boards on the dross, barely illuminated by the dormer window, the old man measured the attic's darkness until the opening of the exit, shimmering with dense streams of light, quietly emerged from around a corner.

The old man walked out into the light and quickly covered his eyes with his sleeve. Painfully the darkness left his eyes.

\* \* \*

"Is anyone there?"

"...there?"

"Isn't anyone there?" Romanikha stood at the door of the service entrance, yelling into the booming, black void. She was afraid to go farther, though she told herself that she was not scared, and that she would follow her husband wherever he went.

The house, with its roof caved in, rustled and cracked. It was silent, only the plaster poured down. It was empty all around her. The tenants who had been spared, and the tenants of neighboring buildings, were afraid to come near the house. It was just about to collapse, it was barely standing.

Romanikha called her husband and waited in vain. She got no answer. Her husband was silent, though he was here somewhere. No answer. She had to go to him herself, into the black void, but she could not.

"Is anyone there?"

"...there?"

"Isn't anyone there?" No matter how she tried, she could not call her husband by name. She knew that she was calling him wrong, doing it all wrong, but she could not call his name, just as she could not go any farther.

Something tapped behind her, outside. Someone was coming, stepping heavily. She turned around—a female corpse stood behind her.

"Marusia." was all Romanikha said. There was no more air, there was nothing more to say.

"Follow me," Marusia breathed out heavily and slowly, as if the earth of the grave pressed her throat. She stepped forward, and just as slowly as her steps had tapped on the pavement, the words fell from the darkness. "He won't come. He just died, no one killed him. Only the murdered, those tormented with injustice will rise from the grave. Only the slain innocents cry out for Judgement."

"But he came, he came to me himself..." Romanikha hastened to explain, to tell her everything quickly. She was afraid that Marusia would leave her alone.

"He was looking for the lilac leaf that you forgot to put in his coffin, he came for that."

And then Romanikha remembered how the dying man had begged, how he had cried a last, slow tear, and talked about the leaf. She had promised then to put the leaf with him, the very one he had torn off beneath the window and pressed to his lips. But she just forgot. Everything collapsed on top of her. So many forms alone, how many documents she had to fill out! How could she remember the leaf? Romanikha remembered and cried quietly. She followed Marusia.

They left together, with a hollow and high-pitched echo.

\* \* \*

Looking around, the old man figured that he was getting there, but that he had to get up higher, much higher. Now he was in the lower part of the eight-sided tower that crowned the huge building, and he had to climb up inside that tower to the very top, where the spire started.

A wind blew down from the vaults and dark arches, throwing bits of fine pigeon feathers in his face, sweeping dry pigeon droppings from the slate. Wiping the dust from his face, the old man made out that the rows of arches were all crowded with birds, all the cornices and vaults that closely surrounded the main tower and connected it to four small towers at its corners. Every ledge, every hollow in the stone bristled with doves, gray as rat's fur. Only the slate of the floor, spattered with droppings, was a bit more open, and only a few big dirty birds walked up and down.

"There it is, the bird of peace," the old man thought gloomily and watched as they shot up in a swift-scudding cloud and rushed by the walls in a thunderous flapping of wings.

The old man walked through the huge arch to the very edge of the platform and looked down. Right below him, on the roof of the residential part of the building, a whole crowd of tenants were settled. From below, behind the stone parapet, they could not be seen, but they were set up comfortably and safely on the wide roof, faced with granite slabs. Several people noticed the old man.

"Hey, gramps!" one yelled. "What are you doing up there?"

They all turned towards the old man, and he lost his head, and froze beneath the gaze of the tenants.

"Come on down here, gramps—you're not allowed up there!" yelled the fellow who had first noticed the old man. His voice reverberated off the stone walls, rang sharply in the arches, scaring the pigeons.

"I know what's allowed without your telling me," the old man could not resist yelling back. The fellow down below instantly got angry.

"Get down, I said!"

"Leave him alone, Efim," a beautiful, slightly languid-looking girl said to the fellow. Another one, skinny and fidgety, stuck up for her. "What did he do to you?"

"But what's he doing..." he railed on.

While they distracted the fellow, the old man hurried out of sight and stuck his nose through the attic door again to find a stairway up. He did not like those people, and not because that fellow was pestering him—it takes all kinds—but because it was so peaceful for them there. The wind didn't even blow. How could they possibly notice Woe behind walls like that? How could they feel Fear, or know Misfortune? They could not care less about the slaughtered innocents, about those who rose from the grave. And they could not care less about the Evil One—they would make peace with him happily.

The old man climbed higher and higher up the dark stairway, barely lighted through the thick, dusty glass of the windows, round, or narrow lancets. He climbed past vibrating machines, which shone with dim lamps, pumped water and drew in an endless cable covered with thick, black grease. He climbed past humming iron electrical shields with red lightning bolts and white skulls, past thick black cables.

Yet another door. Not even a door, but a small hatchway. The old man threw it open, and a wind, a strong wind, howled, burst into the tower, so high above the earth. In a tangle of wires, cramp-irons led straight from the hatchway to the star itself. The spire seemed thin in the high, gray air, and the cramp-irons insecure.

"If they're iron," the old man thought, "they've probably rusted through—they'll break in the middle." The cramp-irons turned out to be copper, firmly fixed in green copper plates. "If just one of those suns comes out now and flares up, starts blazing away, I won't be able to see a thing," the old man thought, and still could not decide. But the suns were gone, clouds covered them. A storm approached.

The old man left the box by the hatchway, pulled out only one saw and wound a wire around it to attach it to his belt. He stood a moment longer, sighed and, crossing himself—crossing himself for the first time in his life, with a fervent sign—began climbing quickly.

The wind tore at him, but the old man hung on, and climbed higher and higher, up to the star itself. Now he had reached the narrow platform. The star was right there, pressing against his head with its dark glass in a brass frame. It was empty all around him, so empty and unstable that the city below and the whole earth vanished somewhere. Only the sphere that topped the spire hung in the air, huge and slippery, smelling sourly of brass. The star was on a steel pin above the sphere. A cable was bolted to one of its lower rays, to its brass frame, and lashed to the handrail of the platform. It ran inside between the plates.

"I'll stand on this side," the old man decided. He got up, untied the saw and stretched out so that his chest leaned full against the sphere. Rasping, he hacked away at the pin.

At once everything started spinning around him. It seemed to the old man that he was falling, slipping down the bulge of the sphere and flying, flying down. But no, waiting a moment he understood that it was not he, but the sphere itself, the whole pin, together with the huge, heavy star, made by no human hand, that was trembling, swinging loose in the empty air.

He hacked hard once again and started sawing with short jerks. The narrow saw went deeper and deeper into the hard steel. "That's it!" The old man was happy and did not notice the mad wind nearby, did not notice how the pin of the huge building quivered. The old man sawed, and the thin strip of steel cut him off from salvation.

Suddenly the whole platform pitched so that the old man barely held on, grabbing the cable with his free hand. Across the whole city, Front and Victory came straight towards him. A huge Front, a collosal Victory. Both drunk, intoxicated with blood. One more step and they would be on top of him. The old man was lost, and everyone else with him. There is no salvation, and there will be none.

The old man stopped and lowered his saw. And everything quivered once again. Fear appeared from the other direction, smoky and black, as if half the city were burning. On the right rose Woe, and on the left Misfortune ascended. They covered the old man like a black wall, and lightning gleamed, glittering nearby.

He was sawing again, quickly and hurriedly, bathed in sweat. "I wish this were a pipe and not a solid bar," he thought quickly, though he knew that the bar was too thin to be hollow. "But maybe it really is a pipe." He thought and thought, and even saw that the huge star that had rolled so slowly at first shook faster now, tearing from its body the thick copper lathe by which the cable was screwed on. Its edge struck the plates of the spire, strewing heavy shards of ruby-colored glass. It roared, and thundered fiercely down.

He saw everything flooded with light, and not from three, but from one bright sun. When it is summer—it is summer, and in winter—it is winter. In the city there were no dreadful buildings with bloody stars that peeled and stared down from the spires like cockroach eyes. There were no fronts, and no more victories, even peaceful ones. Fear did not soar like a black fire, woe did not rise, and misfortune would never again ascend. And the bell in that white church outside of town rings with a bright, joyful sound. The small bells chime in, echo happily, and others answer them—silver ones that live quietly in everyone's breast...

\* \* \*

Suddenly the sky above the old man struck and split. A fiery river engulfed him. His tarpaulin jacket, wet from the rain, burst into fierce flames. And the old man saw the Evil One in his blazing red shirt descending. The Evil One stood next to him and grinned. "Don't bother, old man. While there are men—there will be fronts. While there are men—there will be victories. And I—shall be!" The old man saw no more. Dropping his saw, he fell. An old man in a burning tarpaulin jacket fell on the heavy, red granite.

\* \* \*

"What's going on here?"

"Well, comrade officer, some half-witted old man fell down from up there—struck by lightning."

"Why'd he climb up there?"

"Who knows with a half-wit?" The yardman shrugged his shoulders. "He's not in our co-op. Looks like he was sawing something. See over there, there's a hacksaw." And he pointed to the broken saw, lying right by the road.

"Did he say anything?"

"He talked a little—about some holiday, three suns of some kind... Just all sorts of nonsense..."

"He was crazy," the policeman concluded, and he looked at the sky, where a storm cloud thundered as it left the city, and a damp sun, bright after the storm, struck the star on the shining spire. "Okay, now we'll write up a report."

"Hey, Artishchev!" they called from a police van which braked jauntily on the wet macadem. "Come on, quit writing, you can do it later."

"What's going on?"

"A building collapsed over on the corner."

"Which one?"

"The gray one with the chimney."

"Many dead?"

"A few. One old woman was killed. Let's go dig them out, maybe we'll find someone else and get ourselves a bonus."

"You will." Artishchev grinned. "Okay, I'm coming."

And on the stones lay a dead old man who wanted to save the city, but could not. He looked now with lifeless eyes. And in them—three suns hung above the city, as they will always hang; in them it was a holiday, as it will be forever now, until Judgement Day—a Red holiday.

*1973-1975*
*Moscow*

# NOTES

## PART I

### Chapter One

1. High-quality Soviet-made products manufactured for export—furs, rugs, folk art, liquor—are offered for sale to foreign tourists in *Beryozka* shops. Because of the chronic shortages of many goods, the shop clerks enjoy a glamorous and lucrative position. An enterprising *Beryozka* employee may trade merchandise in this shop for other hard-to-get items through a network of acquaintances: meat and vegetables from a grocery store clerk, Western medicines from a hospital worker, concert tickets from a musician. Because of the possibilities for outright black market activity and the constant exposure to foreigners, a security clearance is required for *Beryozka* employees.

2. The Committee on State Security, the KGB.

### Chapter Two

1. Victory Day.

2. Living space, measured in square meters, is allocated according to the number of persons in a family unit, and is limited by law. It is a tradeable commodity, and Dmitry could use the space to which he is legally entitled in a deal that might force his wife to split up their apartment.

### Chapter Four

1. Belomor Canal cigarettes, a Soviet brand, have cardboard mouthpieces running half their length. The low-quality paper used makes them look gray.

2. Soviet beerhalls sell smoked fish and dark bread, the traditional "chaser" for serious beer-drinking.

### Chapter Five

1. "Overfulfilling the plan" is a cliché of Soviet rhetoric indicating production beyond expected capacity. It looks good in central planning offices, is lucrative to all concerned and is easily achieved by underestimating production capabilities in the first place. There is an annual year-end drive for overfulfillment. If production quotas are met a few days ahead of schedule, a plant may close early for New Year's vacation.

2. City workers are regularly required to do "volunteer" work on collective farms *(kolkhozy)* at harvest time. Willingness to engage in, and

organize such community projects *(obshchestvennaia rabota)*, as well as involvement in the Komsomol (the Communist Youth League) can play an important role in advancement or in admission to universities.

3. Sausage is the only meat available with any regularity in Russia. Since the distribution of food, like everything else, is centralized, the selection is much better in large cities.

4. Communal apartments, still common even in Moscow and Leningrad, consist of three or four rooms, each housing one family unit, and a common kitchen, bathroom, and toilet. Neighbors normally post a duty schedule indicating who is responsible for cleaning in a given week.

5. The stock heroes of Socialist Realist novels are the Party activists—square-jawed, selfless, just and wise—who right wrongs, educate the people, and move the coutry towards Communism.

6. Weekly literary newspaper published by the Union of Writers of the USSR.

## PART II

### *Chapter One*

1. Pensions are at best an income supplement. Even undergraduates, who live at home or in rent-free dormitories and eat in state-subsidized cafeterias, receive a monthly stipend of 35-40 rubles. Older citizens often find low-paying jobs as janitors, watchmen, or cafeteria workers after mandatory retirement.

2. The tag phrase for major show-case construction sites built with prison-camp laborers and idealistic Komsomol volunteers.

### *Chapter Two*

1. The Committee on State Security, the KGB.

2. A sepulchre with niches for cinerary urns. In Russian cemeteries, the slabs covering the niches, as well as gravestones or crosses, often bear both an inscription and a photograph of the deceased.

3. Work brigades of Komsomol members set up in various enterprises to stimulate production.

4. A worker who voluntarily assists the Party in its activities and policies, and encourages his colleagues to cooperate with Party directives.

### *Chapter Three*

1. Holiday decorations include portraits mounted in parks and on major public buildings. Currently, the portraits are of Marx, Engels, and

Lenin; earlier, Stalin was one of the trinity.

2. Well-orchestrated "spontaneous" displays of patriotism on the anniversary of the October Revolution (November 7), and Comintern Day (May 1).

3. A snack bar offering cheese, fish, or sausage sandwiches, ice cream, and liquor. This is an alternative to a restaurant meal—easily a whole evening's entertainment. Buffets operate in concert halls, research libraries, clubs, hotels, and factories.

**LIBRARY OF DAVIDSON COLLEGE**